SYLVESTER STALLONE

DAYLIGHT

UNIVERSAL PICTURES PRESENTS A DAVIS ENTERTAINMENT / JOSEPH M. SINGER PRODUCTION

A ROB COHEN FILM "DAYLIGHT" AMY BRENNEMAN VIGGO MORTENSEN

DAN HEDAYA JAY O SANDERS KAREN YOUNG CLAIRE BLOOM BARRY NEWMAN

AND STAN SHAW MUSIC BY RANDY EDELMAN CO-EXECUTIVE PRODUCER PAUL NEESAN

EDITED BY PETER AMUNDSON PRODUCTION DESIGNER BENJAMIN FERNANDEZ DIRECTOR OF PHOTOGRAPHY DAVID EGGBY A.C.S.

CO-PRODUCER HESTER HARGETT EXECUTIVE PRODUCER RAFFAELLA DE LAURENTIIS WRITTEN BY LESLIE BOHEM

PRODUCED BY JOHN DAVIS JOSEPH M. SINGER DAVID T. FRIENDLY

SPECIAL VISUAL EFFECTS AND ANIMATION BY INDUSTRIAL LIGHT & MAGIC   DIRECTED BY ROB COHEN

DTS STEREO IN SELECTED THEATERS   DIGITAL dts SOUND

 A UNIVERSAL RELEASE UNIVERSAL AN MCA COMPANY

DAYLIGHT

A NOVEL BY
MAX ALLAN COLLINS

BASED ON THE MOTION PICTURE WRITTEN BY
LESLIE BOHEM

BOULEVARD BOOKS, NEW YORK

DAYLIGHT

A novel by Max Allan Collins, based on a screenplay written by Leslie Bohem.

A Boulevard Book / published by arrangement with MCA Publishing Rights, a Division of MCA, Inc.

PRINTING HISTORY
Boulevard edition/December 1996

The Putnam Berkley World Wide Web site address is
http://www.berkley.com/berkley

ISBN: 1-57297-155-X

BOULEVARD
Boulevard Books are published by The Berkley Publishing Group,
200 Madison Avenue, New York, New York 10016.
BOULEVARD and its logo are trademarks
belonging to Berkley Publishing Corporation.

PRINTED IN THE UNITED STATES OF AMERICA

10 9 8 7 6 5 4 3 2

For Rick Marcus and Mike Dominic—
Eagles who dare

"Give me a ship for I intend to go in harm's way."
—ADMIRAL JOHN PAUL JONES
(motto inscribed on a plaque
above the desk of
Deputy Chief Paul Maniscalco of the
Emergency Medical Services
of the City of New York)

"The light at the end of the tunnel could be a train."
—ANONYMOUS

DAYLIGHT

PROLOGUE

Disasters such as the explosion in the Manhattan Tunnel hide a small but important blessing within their worlds of misfortune: they serve to remind us of our common humanity. In the soot-smudged features of victims, and survivors, we see countenances that could easily belong to our brothers, sisters, fathers, mothers, sons, daughters.

And even as we ask how men could be so inhuman as to purposely or (as in the instance of the Manhattan Tunnel explosion) carelessly endanger the lives of so many innocents, we are confronted by the selflessness, the heroism, of rescue workers and game bystanders who risk their lives in seeking to save those of strangers.

Not everyone involved in the Manhattan Tunnel explosion was available for the purposes of the documentary-in-prose you are about to read. Many of them did not survive. A few others have books or movie deals of their own that present a conflict with this project.

But it is my hope that these personal reminiscences of survivors will serve to make more real for readers a disaster that the media has painted larger than life. For those who experienced it, the Manhattan Tunnel explosion was an all-too-intimate encounter with death.

—M.A.C.

1

"A" AS IN APPLE

The Manhattan Tunnel, of course, is one of the main arteries connecting the island of Manhattan with the rest of the country. Even at non-rush-hour times, the stream of cars is steady. On the day of the disaster, as on any prior day, few if any of the ninety-thousand-plus citizens who drove through that shaft gave even a moment's thought to the incredible feat of engineering that allowed them to pass, coolly and dryly, beneath seventy-two feet of the Hudson River, not to mention twenty-four feet of sludgy riverbed.

The man-made wonder of the Manhattan Tunnel began inauspiciously as a design scribbled on a napkin in a Manhattan tavern in 1918. Edward Trammel's vision came to life in 1921 when thousands of Irish immigrants, dubbed "sandhogs," began to dig. Nine million dollars and thirty-seven lives later, the Manhattan Tunnel was open to the public.

In all those years it had never closed—until November 28 of last year.

Imagine, if you will, that afternoon, an afternoon cold yet sunny, as George Tyrell—husky, affable Afro-American in the light blue shirt and navy trousers of a Transit Authority cop—boards a Tri-State Transit Authority van idling at the curb near the tunnel entrance on the Manhattan side, beneath a towering, magnificent Art Deco statue of a robed woman. Tyrell blows her a kiss, boards the van, and greets his brother officers with grins and high fives; Tyrell likes his job, and his fellow workers.

Rubber cones have been positioned to funnel traffic into one lane, a temporary measure that allows the van to make its numerous shift-change stops along the catwalk within the tunnel, dropping the tunnel and bridge officers at the various glass booths along the catwalk.

Soon Tyrell is let out at his post. He high-fives the cop he's replacing, but does not immediately go inside his glass booth. Instead, Tyrell positions himself on the elevated sidewalk under the video surveillance camera and begins to gesture as he speaks into his walkie-talkie.

GRACE LINCOLN

I was at the communications desk, you know, in the control room. It's pretty cramped in there, a little network of cubbyholes, little beehive of activity, desks and chairs all jammed together. Not exactly high-tech, neither. Our monitors are black-and-white, but I suppose the powers-that-be figure, who needs color in a tunnel? We're not exactly watching VH-1. We got different episodes of the same program playing on thirty-six screens, looking at different views of the North Tunnel, the South Tunnel.

Anyway, I been going with George Tyrell for over a year. He was after me a lot longer than that, and while there wasn't a rule against employees dating, there was a departmental no-fraternization-on-the-job policy. And I like to be professional, you know, so I kept putting him off. But he knew I liked him, because I put him off in that teasing way that says you're not really putting 'em off, you know what I'm saying?

Every morning he would say hello to me, so it was no surprise seeing his face staring up at me on my monitor, but his grin, you know, it was goofier than usual. Like the cat that ate the canary.

Doesn't embarrass me, at this point, to admit it, George and me a couple, but we were at work at the time, and the fact that I spent last night at his apartment wasn't something I wanted to put on a billboard, you know what I'm saying?

But there he is, grinning, dangling something sparkly like it's a shiny worm he's going to put on a hook. Then I recognize it: it's that gold bracelet he bought me for my birthday. Gaudy damn thing I wouldn't even wear if my man hadn't picked it out for me.

"Look what I found under my bed, sugar," George is saying.

He wasn't the only one with a walkie-talkie. I said into mine, "You think you could be a little less discreet?"

"Suppose if I really tried."

That goofy smile of his, it was a great smile really, made me smile back. Couldn't be mad at that big clown.

"I'll see you after work," I said, kind of quiet.

"What? Speak up! Can't hear you over the traffic."

He just wanted to embarrass me, get the rest of them in the control room to hear me sweet-talking him and give me a bad time. He was a devil, that George.

"You heard me, all right," I said, but I was smiling.

"I'm countin' the hours, sugar," he said.

Then I just got back to work. Routine, watching views of the two tunnels on my black-and-white TVs, sometimes bringing something up for a closer look on my main, bigger-screen monitor, if something seemed out of the ordinary.

But nothing much did.

It seemed like just another day.

"FRANK SMITH"
(real name withheld by request)

You think I like working inside the chemical asshole of Connecticut? Smokestacks steaming filth into the sky? People like me, that work at places like this, we die of cancer before we get our retirement bennies. But I got a family, I got to work, and I make no apologies. Maybe I don't sleep so good at night, after what happened in that tunnel, but I ain't quit my job. My family comes first. Look out for number one.

It was just another run, another midnight dumping haul. Three trucks, a convoy of them, come in past the railroad siding down inside and through the main warehouse, it's this brick mother that's been there since Jesus was a baby, and they pull up along the canal. Lots of barges are tethered there, and you know what they're loaded with: sulfurous chemical shit.

Half a dozen forklifts caravaned out these double-tiered pallets of yellow plastic canisters; they didn't have Tang in them, believe you me. I directed some of the guys to start loading the trucks, then I went over to the head driver.

"The gate'll be open from eleven to midnight," I tell him. "Just get to Jersey on time."

This guy has five o'clock shadow that makes Nixon look clean-shaven. He has eyes deader and blacker than asphalt.

8

He doesn't say a word, he just holds out his hand and I put the envelope of cash in it. He's counting the cash when we hear a crash behind us.

I about soiled my shorts, and this hard-ass truck driver, he had the expression of a scared little girl.

A pallet of those damn poison canisters had slipped from one of the forklift tongues, but the lids were still on good and tight. The guy operating the forklift looked sheepish, said, "Sorry," and I said, "Sorry don't cut it."

But I let it go at that, and everybody kind of breathed easy and they went back to loading.

The trucker is riffling through the bills in the envelope and he kind of smirks and says, "Lunch money. A run like this and I get fuckin' lunch money."

"Here's a thought," I say. "Change careers."

He grunts at me, pocketing the envelope.

"Just be there by midnight," I say. "Catch you next Friday. It's like those potato chips. You run out, we'll make more."

Seemed pretty funny at the time.

MADELYNE THOMPSON

The Big Apple, they call it. Why not the Big Rathole? They could hire Disney to design a real cute furry rodent for the billboards and T-shirts; have animated commercials. Oh, sure, people are used to the Big Apple designation, you wouldn't want to make the transition too soon. You could start gradually, maybe with a picture of a rat with an apple in its mouth.

With an imagination like this, you'd think I'd be published by now, or produced. I moved to New York from the Midwest to log some "life experience," like my mentor back at the University of Iowa Writers Workshop suggested I get, if I ever really wanted to be a playwright instead of just talking about it.

And, of course, a playwright needed to be close to the heart of the theatrical world, and that was NYC, right? Broadway. Off-Broadway. Off-off-Broadway . . .

But that was almost ten years ago, and what had I learned? That afternoon, before I made my decision, I was maneuvering down a snowy sidewalk in the war zone I laughingly referred to as "my neighborhood," loaded down with a sack of groceries and, of course, my canvas manuscript bag.

And I had acquired *some* skills, in my tour of NYC duty: I could nimbly step over a sprawled, passed-out junkie with the best of them. You learn to move quickly if you're a young (reasonably young) attractive (reasonably attractive) woman in this city; another skill. And another: I could slot my key in the door of my tenement building with one hand even while keeping an eye over one shoulder to make sure some more alert junkie didn't shoulder his way into my palace.

My apartment was a railroad flat—four locks on the door, tub in the kitchen, toilet in the hall, and the rent was only seven hundred a month. A steal. For the landlord. I put my groceries on the counter and had a look at the mail. A letter I'd been waiting for sent an excited chill up my spine and I was grinning eagerly as I tore it open.

But what I read was: *Dear Mr. Thompson, thank you for your submission. Regretfully at this time we blah blah blah. . . .*

Mister Thompson yet. How carefully could they have read my play if they were misinterpreting my damn *byline*?

I wadded up the rejection slip, gave it a basketball toss toward the circular file, missing by a mile.

Then I ran some hot tap water, picking up a *Les Miz* mug

from the sink; two roaches from under the cup scurried down the sink, to a safer haven. I envied them. I filled my cup, plunked in a tea bag. Herbal.

My office, if you could call it an office, was in the kitchen, if you could call it a kitchen, and on the table, my laptop—the neatly stacked pages of Act One alongside—was waiting patiently for me to switch it on and make magic. The theatrical posters on the walls—Mamet, Rabe, Sondheim, a vintage Maxwell Anderson (*The Bad Seed*)—encouraged me not to give up.

I sat. Switched on the machine. Its amber screen glowed blankly but warmly, encouragingly, at me. I cracked my knuckles. Poised fingertips above keys . . .

The phone rang. But I would not be interrupted. Art took precedence over commerce.

Because who else would be calling me but somebody from work, wanting me to fill in? It sure as hell wasn't a guy; I hadn't had a date in months. Art took precedence over that, too.

"You there, Mad?" the answering machine asked.

It was Kimberly.

"It's Kimberly," the answering machine said. "Honey, I know it's short notice, but could you take my shift today?"

"No fucking way," I said.

"I already told Julio you would," the answering machine said, "so it's sort of a done deal. Counting on you, sweetie. Owe ya one. Bye!"

Cheap shot. If she wanted to assume I'd cover for her, that was her damn problem. We're tough in New York City. We don't push around easy.

I typed in a machine-gun burst: *Act Two. Lights up on* . . .

I stopped, frowned. "On what?"

A blare of salsa music from the apartment above goosed me. It wasn't any louder than a symphony of jackhammers.

I looked up at the ceiling, wondering why it wasn't pulsing. When I looked back down at my laptop keyboard, a roach was making its way slowly across the keys.

I slapped him to hell and gone with my pocket thesaurus—*gotcha!*—and my computer squawked like *it* was what got squashed.

The phone rang again. I typed: . . . *an upscale apartment on Central Park West* . . .

"Hey, Shakespeare!" a male voice said from the answering machine, a voice rising above restaurant clatter, not to mention the salsa sounds from above.

It was Julio.

"It's Julio!" the answering machine said. "Kim said you're taking her shift and I need you down here five minutes ago! We're dyin' down here!"

I sighed, saved what I'd written (it would be tragic to lose so much good work), and shut off the computer. Picked up the phone and told Julio not to get his panties in a bunch. I'd be right there. Like Scotty beamed me over.

Unbuttoning my dress as quickly as tearing off an inspired sentence on the laptop keys, I moved to my packed closet and pulled out a dainty ensemble—black skirt, wing-collar shirt, black bow tie—suitable for the chorus line of a road-show of *Cabaret*, or for my dumb waitress job, flipped the clothes onto my unmade daybed, pulled open my top dresser drawer, and screamed.

There, nestled lovingly amidst my best Victoria's Secret lingerie (given so little use of late), was a rat no larger than a pit bull. He gazed at me with his fearless little arrogant New York rat eyes, baring healthier-looking teeth than I'd seen in days.

So the little bastard thought *he* was tough?

I yanked the police-lock bar from my door and I smashed it into the drawer, and speared that hairy son of a bitch again, and again, and again, and again, and then shut the drawer with my body.

Then I stood there, panting, and when I glanced at the dresser mirror, the eyes that looked back at me were wild, crazed, and a face that had once been deemed pretty enough to be that of a homecoming queen finalist in LaPorte, Indiana, was contorted in a mask of rage.

A siren wailed outside. Cops? Fire? Or the loony-bin boys, come to take me for a much-needed rest?

I laughed at myself, then looked at the bloody, hairy police-lock bar in my hand and dropped it like a red-hot poker.

That was when I made the decision. At any other time, at any other moment, it would have been the right one, too. If it just hadn't been that moment.

''I'm outta here,'' I said.

Nobody ever packed faster. And before you know it, I'm in my clunker car, my measly car stereo blaring *La Traviata* while I'm singing my own version of ''New York, New York'' at the top of my lungs.

Start spreadin' the news, I'm leavin' today—I'm fed up to here with it. . . .

That's exactly what I was singing when I entered that tunnel. It felt good knowing that New York wasn't on the other side.

NILES BANCROFT

The funny thing is, at work, none of us wore any of the clothing from our catalogs. Expensive as the Territory Beyond apparel line was, it was far too casual for a boardroom. We were strictly a Hugo Boss bunch. Young. Athletic. Multiracial. We were everything but solvent.

Right now we sat in the sleek, darkened boardroom watching a ninety-second roll of the dice the company's future hinged on. On the big-screen TV, a ruggedly handsome modern-day Marlboro Man jogged across the dunes as the sun set. His Arab-style headgear was emblazoned with our logo: TERRITORY BEYOND. Then, in quickly edited, almost subliminal bursts, the same virile figure, always in Territory Beyond khaki and sheepskin and other stuff of ours, climbed a frozen waterfall with pitons and pickaxes; kayaked down the Colorado River; snowboarded down a chute at Vail; Roller Bladed in Mussolini's stadium; spelunked the Csardis Cave; and reached the summit of Mount Rainier, just in time to turn to the camera and say: "Territory Beyond—it's still out there!"

And finally the same figure, back on the ocher dunes, jogged directly into the perfect orange orb of a digitally rendered sun, with our slogan—"It's Still Out There"—supered over.

Enthusiastic applause accompanied the lights coming up.

The man at the end of the table, closest to the screen, swiveled around and flashed a grin. He was the man in the commercial. He was our boss, our fearless leader, Roy Nord.

"It's exhausting, being me," he said.

We laughed at that. Probably too hard, but Roy liked approval. Expected it, too.

"Guys," he said, "the spot is great. For the dough we spent, it should be." More laughter around the table, nervous this time. "When do we go out with it?"

Bob Ramis, from marketing, said, "Sales are off nineteen percent, Roy."

Roy wanted to be called Roy, not Mr. Nord.

Bob continued: "Midwest is flat, East Coast is soft."

"No positives, Bob?"

Roy liked positives.

Bob smiled weakly. "The new lines are strong in California, and the Northwest."

"I know our market shares, Bob—and we've always been strong in those regions. What I asked was, when do we go out with this killer spot?"

Bob swallowed; he seemed nervous as he answered: "Super Bowl. Halftime."

"Christ," Roy said. "That's a million for thirty seconds."

Jack Tailor, the company treasurer, said, "It's a gamble, Roy. But you've said it so many times yourself. . . ."

"Sometimes you have to gamble."

There were nods all around the table.

Roy was looking out the window. He had a faraway expression. Then swiveled back and snapped: "Then roadblock it. All three networks."

Bob said, "But, Roy—why bother with other networks? The numbers are with the Super Bowl. That's the point. . . ."

"Compared to what we're paying for the Super Bowl spot," Roy said, eyes shining, "it'll take pennies to nail down the other two networks. Hell, check on the superstations, Atlanta, Chicago, anybody with commercial time for sale. If they channel-surf during *my* spot, they'll still see my smiling face."

The execs all around were smiling, nodding, me right along with them. This was what made Roy Nord a great man: he wasn't just a dreamer, he was a doer.

He stood up and smoothed his suit—his Hugo Boss was the nicest, most expensive in the room, though the vicuña topcoat that Jonno was suddenly helping him into *was* out of our catalog. (Jonno was Roy's thick-chested English factum factotum, who seemed to materialize at Roy's side whenever needed. Kind of like that big black guy that carried Mandrake the Magician's top hat and cloak for him.)

"How are we doing on time?" Roy asked Jonno.

"Traffic's impossible. If we take the tunnel, we'll just make it."

"Then the tunnel it is."

Then Roy did something he always did before he left an executive meeting (and he was always first to go): he gave us this sort of arcane bow. I think he considered it stylish, but really, it was pretty pompous. Not that any of us would ever have told him.

And we did admire him. Really. I know pride was surging through me as I watched him stride purposefully toward the door.

Roy Nord was one of a kind, all right. And that Super Bowl commercial, as it turned out, did put Territory Beyond through the roof.

But that was later.

ROGER TRILLING

Eleanor and I had been married twenty-five years last February. We were married on Valentine's Day. Storybook wedding. Storybook marriage, too, for the longest time. We never wanted for anything. Eleanor's family had money, and as a corporate attorney with Allison, Conlon and Ekhardt, I wasn't exactly worrying about where my next meal was coming from.

But there hadn't been a lot of affection in our lives, not since Jonathan passed away. Jonathan was our son, our only child. He was a gifted boy, very talented, and he had an adventurous streak, which I never had. He used to kid me about being stodgy. Why didn't I take a leave of absence and join him, backpacking across Europe? That was a suggestion he made right after college; he had a degree in law, but he never went into practice.

And I never went backpacking.

Though he never stopped asking. Right before he left for

Nepal . . . but I'm wandering. You asked me about that day. It was normal, too normal. Eleanor was fussing over Cooper. He was our other child.

No, I'm being sarcastic. I loved Cooper, I suppose. And people do love dogs, no question about it. Childless couples commonly substitute a pet like Cooper for the child they never had. My problem was, Eleanor substituted Cooper for the child we *had* had, and that seemed sad, and even a little sick.

I tried to talk to her about it, once—two, almost three years ago. She stiffened up. We haven't had normal, intimate relations since. All of her affection was lavished upon that dog. I wasn't jealous of the mutt. It wasn't his fault. I would've taken the affection, if I'd been in his place. If I'd had it that good.

Take, for example, that afternoon. What the hell kind of veterinary has his offices at Eighty-eighth and Fifth Avenue? Right. An expensive goddamn veterinary. The kind that has a brass plaque by the entrance: HERBERT TARNOWER, DVM.

Cooper, who didn't like being poked and probed any more than anybody else who goes for a medical exam, was whining and straining at his leash as we waited for the light to change.

"Easy, boy," I soothed him. "We'll be home 'fore you know it."

"You're hurting him," Eleanor said.

"Dear, if I don't restrain him, he'll run under a cab, and I don't have to be Herbert Tarnower, DVM, to know that would hurt him worse."

"Your sarcasm is disturbing Cooper, dear."

"Traffic and a million New Yorkers are disturbing him."

We began to cross the street. Cooper strained at the leash. I thought about releasing him, just letting him go, pictured him striding through traffic, leash dangling like a second tail. . . .

I did love Cooper. I didn't want him to be hit by a car or anything. I just thought maybe he would have enjoyed a little freedom, himself.

So we took him for a stroll in Central Park on that sunny winter afternoon.

After a time I said, "Dear, do you think that whatever good that specialist may have done might be undone by a long car trip? Maybe we should board him. . . ."

"I would sooner put you in one of those awful cages."

That went without saying.

"Dear," I continued, "he *hates* riding in the car, it puts him off his food for days."

"What are you suggesting, Roger? That we take him back to that quack in Colt's Neck?"

I paused to make my point; Cooper strained at the leash again, eyeing a tree. "Dr. York is perfectly capable. Besides, Eleanor, no one's ever really found anything *wrong* with the dog."

"I *know* he's ill," she said, bending to stroke him. "Mothers know these things."

So we took him along. We were to spend the weekend with her sister Margaret in Colt's Neck, and Margaret is older than Eleanor, and a widow, and a stay-at-home, and we'd have the little guest cottage out back, and maybe, just maybe, Eleanor and I could have had some quiet moments together. I had Courier and Ives images of us driving through the wintry countryside, antiquing in little towns, sharing a romantic lunch at some cozy country inn.

It was after dark when we entered the Manhattan Tunnel, Cooper hanging his head out the window of our Mercedes 24O D, tongue lolling.

So much for Cooper hating car trips. He was already having a better time than I was.

BARBARA SMALLEY, M.D.

The convention was at the Peninsula Hotel, and I was standing on the curb, huddling against the cold next to Dr. Samuels, John Samuels, who'd been hitting on me all weekend, as if our both being recently divorced made us instant soul mates. John seemed to figure the way into my heart—if that's what he was trying to get into—was to show off his superior medical knowledge. All male doctors like to play doctor, if you get my meaning. They all like to show off the size of their stethoscopes.

John had invited me to share the Lincoln Town Car he'd booked for the airport run and, frankly, scored better points with me that way than with his silly medical one-upmanship.

We were in the middle of John trying to impress me when the Lincoln rolled up.

"Lewis is saying to hyperventilate in the case of head injury," John was saying. "Of course, the goal here is to obtain normocapnea. . . ."

That's when I noticed this Kit Latura you've heard so much about. I had no idea what his name was then, of course; only later, when I saw the coverage on TV, read the papers, did I put a name to the face and form. At that moment he was only a limo driver in black uniform and cap with white shirt; but he had the sort of darkly handsome good looks that made me instantly tune out John's medical babble.

I guess it was his eyes that caught you; somehow they had this brooding quality mixed with humor. He had a kind of permanent smirk, but there was nothing smart-ass about him. And he wasn't as big as you might think, from reading about all those things he did. He had a hunk's build, all right, but mainly Latura had a lithe quality, a dancer's grace.

I didn't notice this all at once, of course. At this moment all he was doing was coming around the limo, checking his order slip, saying to John, "Six-thirty flight out of Newark. Gonna be tight."

John said, "There's a fifty-buck tip in it for you if we make it."

Always trying to impress.

Our driver's smirk widened and an eyebrow raised. "Then fasten your seat belts good and tight, boys and girls. We're about to rock-and-roll."

It was like a rocket launching, when he pulled away from the curb, but you know what? I was never scared. He drove quickly, but his maneuvering was deft and his eyes were searching out every detail of traffic, logging every pedestrian. I settled back in the comfy leather seat, safe, secure. In good hands.

"We ran some tests with cerebral blood flow," I told John, picking up on the thread of our curbside conversation, "while I was at Cornell. The results were inconclusive."

"Lewis is the top man on trauma-related head injury," John said. "I wouldn't dismiss that lightly."

That was when I realized Latura was listening to us; he had adjusted his rearview mirror so he could include us in his information gathering. Our eyes met. With that one glance, Latura scored more points with me than John could have had he done a curbside liver transplant standing on his head.

"Lewis has no sense of priorities," I said to John. But my eyes were locked with the driver's. "His research is sloppy. You're just defending a classmate."

I could tell Latura was smiling now, his eyes crinkling.

So I said to our driver, "Don't tell me *you* went to Harvard, too?"

He glanced over his shoulder, threw us a grin. "Naw. They don't have a night school."

"Just watch the road if you want that tip," John said, too curtly. Then to me he said, "Maybe we should have just hailed a cab. Then we wouldn't be burdened with a driver who speaks English."

A few blocks later, his back to us, Latura said easily, matter-of-factly, "Dr. Anton Friendly demonstrated, back in ninety-three, that hyperventilation can worsen or even cause brain ischemia. Mortality rate in the ER triples over the field rate, y'know, 'cause of the induced periods of hypotension. Play God, you just make matters worse."

Then he glanced back and flashed another grin. "But what do I know? You're the experts."

John didn't say anything, after that.

Not till we got near the tunnel, I mean.

LATONYA WASHINGTON

The man down at the detention center parkin' lot, he be shovin' us up on the Department of Corrections bus. Like we animals. I'm a person. Good person. I believe in God. I don't do no drug. I trick 'cause I got a child to bring up. Ain't easy, be fifteen in a cold town like this. If I put in for child support, they find out my age, they take Nordell away.

That was all I be thinkin' about then, is my son Nordell, and how now that I goin' to juvie, he be turned over to the Social Service. I'm the one trickin', why should Nordell, two years old, go to jail, too?

I don't know these other kids, but they names I pick up on soon enough. Kadeem, he a brother, a mean, tall, strong one, too. Arm robbery. Vincent, good-lookin' greaser, I don't know what he be in for. Pimpin', maybe. Maybe I ought to get close to him for business advancement. Little Rican, Mikey, he don't look no older than thirteen, but he a crack-head, so he be in for stealin', too. Just a bunch of kids in orange prison coveralls headed for the juvie slammer. Think we be better citizens when we come out?

It cold and we be shiverin' only we don't show our fear, none of us, we jus' give the guard the cold eye when he pat us down and check the garbage bag they give for suitcases. They too good to us.

Guard, he pat Kadeem down too hard. Kadeem, he say, "Nobody touch me like that."

Guard, he say, "None your lip. Move on."

Kadeem say, "I'll move on. I'll move on your fuckin' head."

And the guard shove Kadeem, guard say, "Move on!"

Kadeem gave him one badass look, but then the guard, he push the four of us in the back of the bus. Lots of room. Plenty places to pick to sit. Nice and free. 'Cept for when the guard close the wire cage door on us and snap us in.

We just sat there in our own little worlds. I be thinkin' about Nordell. Thinkin' 'bout how much I love him. Thinkin' about how I not be cryin' in front of these kids. They got to respect me, and nobody respect somebody cryin' like a baby.

But inside I was cryin', for my baby. Maybe the other three, they was cryin' inside, too. Anyways, all of us was just sittin' there starin' out the window into nothin', watchin' night fall.

It was dark already, when we entered the tunnel.

In a way it was my own stupid fault. I've been doing business in the Chinatown diamond district since I was in my early twenties. I learned a long time ago that you complete your business before sundown. In this part of town, a man in a business suit with a briefcase chained to his wrist is wearing a neon sign that says ROB ME.

But this was an important client, a client whose business would make my week, my month, so I made the transaction. The owner of the shop padlocked the accordion gate behind me as I walked to my double-parked Cadillac, unlocked it, and was just getting in when they were on me.

Out of nowhere! A pair of them, and they were just kids, early twenties, dirty looking, messy, clothes and hair alike—what's the word my daughter Rebecca uses? Grungy. These two *defined* grungy.

On the other hand, their personal slovenliness didn't extend to their skills as thieves. They took me down swiftly, with military precision. One of them had me in a headlock—his body odor was appalling!—while the other snipped my wrist chain with a bolt cutter. Then my keys were snatched from my hand and I was flung, like a rag doll, to the sidewalk.

One of them shouted, "Let's go," over and over, until it was one blurred nonword.

And I was looking up from the sidewalk at the taillights of my fleeing Cadillac. The entire incident had taken, perhaps, seven seconds.

I had been robbed before. The gem dealer who tells you he hasn't been robbed is a liar. The gem dealer who tells you any robbery isn't a nerve-racking, stomach-churning experience is a damn liar.

But I knew the worst of it was over. I picked myself off the pavement with as much dignity as I could muster—no other pedestrians were offering aid, of course, this being New York—and I dusted myself off, sighed, and withdrew my cell phone from my suitcoat pocket.

I flipped the phone open, punched 911.

I identified myself, gave the location, and said, "My car was just stolen. It's registered with Electroguard, which includes a tracking device. ID number is A as in apple, four-seven-zero-nine."

In a way, I suppose, I'm at least partly to blame for what happened later. I was a part of the chain reaction to follow. But if you think I feel bad about taking precautions, think again. I work in a dangerous business in a dangerous town. What is it my son David says?

Shit happens.

2

FIRESTORM

The magnificent Art Deco sculpture of a robed woman that looked down on four lanes of traffic merging into two was the work of Paul Manship, who also provided several notable Art Moderne sculptures for the 1939 World's Fair, the "World of Tomorrow."

Could those dreamers of a technological utopia have imagined a world where three flatbed trucks loaded down with canisters of toxic, explosive detritus would roll silently, obliviously, past a sign saying, TRANSPORTING OF HAZARDOUS WASTE MATERIALS FORBIDDEN? What would Manship have said had he known his grand Art Deco lady was beckoning three time-bombs-on-wheels into the tunnel she protected?

We can only imagine. Just as we can imagine the confusion and fear of Billy Watson and his friend (and accomplice) Fred Simmons, the "grungy" assailants of gem dealer Robert Goldberg, when the Cadillac's car phone rang and its Port-a-Fax emitted a message.

Only moments before they had surely been euphoric over their haul—can you picture the sea of diamonds drifting over the blue-felt-liner shore within Goldberg's valise? The sparkle of the diamonds would be matched only by that of the eyes of those grungy petty thieves.

And now a fax message was informing them that they were to Stop Now. We have you tracked on Electroguard.

What's that?

Shit! It must tell the cops where we're at!

And when they looked up (and there's no imagining now, but verified reports) the two thieves found themselves looking directly at a police squad car coming right at them. As if to underscore the obvious, the squad car's siren popped on.

The boy behind the wheel, Watson, threw the Caddy in reverse; but another squad car was coming up fast behind them, boxing them in.

Give Billy Watson credit: he was (as his prior criminal record later indicated) nothing if not a skilled "wheelman," and when he backed up, and turned, he timed it perfectly so that the two squad cars slammed into each other.

The officers in the two cars (none of whom was seriously injured) reported two further facts: Fred Simmons whooped with glee, and the Cadillac flew away, down Canal Street.

ASHLEY CRIGHTON

First of all, I may only be fourteen, but I am definitely the most mature one in my family. My father, Steven, is an editor with a New York publishing house. My mother, Sarah, is a teacher of music at a private school in Manhattan. Neither one of them makes a lot of money, but as a two-income household, we don't starve or anything.

Don't they sound like grown-up, responsible citizens?

Think again.

My dad has a ponytail and an earring and he thinks if he listens to Counting Crows on the radio, I'll think he's cool and he'll convince himself he's not forty-one. My mom is much more conservative, in a liberal sort of way. Not much makeup, or anyway not till lately, after what happened with Dad and that assistant editor he was working with, Linda Hughes.

Lately, Mom has kind of spruced herself up, everything but her attitude. She's like a lot of teachers. She can't leave the bossiness, that know-it-all quality, at school. She's always the expert. On everything. Plus, she can't resist giving Dad the needle.

I can't blame her, Dad messing around on her with some younger woman. Hard to think of Linda as a woman at all. I mean, to me she's just a girl. She's, what? Seven years older than me? I have bigger boobs and I haven't even stopped growing yet, I hope. But Linda's funny and loose and pretty and slim and blond, and while Mom is still kind of pretty, the rest of that, she's the opposite.

I used to like Linda. I used to see her when she came over weekends to work with Dad on manuscripts. Mom and her were friendly, too, though I think Mom was already kind of suspicious. What really made her suspicious, I think, was when Linda *stopped* coming around. And when Dad started going to business conventions and writers' conferences every other weekend or so.

Look, I don't know how Mom and Dad patched it together, but about a month before, they did, or claimed to. They had a big blowup and I just shut my door and put on the headphones (personally, I hate Counting Crows—give me Mariah Carey anytime) and the next morning they were all kissy face. All I thought was, *Yuck,* but I suppose it was better than having to pick one of them to live with.

It seemed to me things had kind of been deteriorating, ever since. Like the night before the tunnel, we had this big knock-down-drag-out about me going on this "family vacation" with them.

At first I tried to reason with them and pretended to be nice. "You two need a romantic getaway, just the two of you—to get to know each other again."

"This isn't a second honeymoon, dear," Mom lectured me sweetly, "it's a family vacation."

"No, it isn't," I said. "We're staying with Dad's old college roommate. What sort of fun is that? I want to stay home. I want to skate at Rockefeller Center. This *sucks*!"

But of course I wound up in the backseat. I did have my 8mm video camera with me. Did I mention I'm going to be a filmmaker? I record stuff—life—and then I edit my own documentaries. You have any idea what kind of *offers* I'm getting for my footage of what happened?

Anyway, I was shooting out the window, catching some street stuff, when Mom started in reading from a guidebook. I mean, we live in New York. What kind of person lives in New York and buys a New York guidebook? An insane person. A parent.

So Mom starts reeling off info about when the tunnel was built, and how some jerk drew it up on a napkin, and how many lives were lost, and, out of nowhere, she says, "Did you and Linda ever go sightseeing? On those business trips?"

Very sweet. And acid.

Dad stiffened at the wheel. I caught this on my camera, by the way. This is real-life drama. You can't write this stuff.

"Sarah, I don't want to talk about Linda. Linda is the past.

My present, my future, is with you and Ashley.''

That seemed like a pretty good comeback to me; kind of dignified, even. Of course, working in the book business, my dad can pull stuff like that out of his butt.

But, naturally, Mom topped him. If he'd been a Ping-Pong ball, he'd have been slammed.

"What can I ever do to repay you?" Mom said sweetly.

I had a feeling Dad was the one going to be doing the paying around here.

Oh, and I got Mom's sarcastic put-down on tape, too. In case I ever want to do a documentary on dysfunctional families or something.

Then the car jerked, real sudden, and I fumbled with my camera, getting kind of a cool *NYPD Blue* shot, I later discovered, on playback—but at the time it just scared me and pissed me off.

"Hey!" I yelled.

"Did you *see* that asshole?" my dad said, sitting forward to where his forehead almost touched the windshield. "Did you see the way he cut me off?"

I wish I had. I wish I'd got it on tape. All I saw was the Cadillac going like a bat out of hell, flying into the cave of the Manhattan Tunnel.

GRACE LINCOLN

My supervisor, Norm Bassett, is a good guy, about ready to retire. He brought in some coffee for both of us and was sitting down, scoping out the monitors right before the caca hit the fan.

"Mind if I tune in the Knicks game?" he asked me.

"Guess that's better than *The Flintstones*," I said, which was his request yesterday.

Then he blurted, "What the hell!"

I turned toward him and he was bent over a monitor, wide-eyed; something bad was going down. . . .

I craned to see: the monitor showed a Cadillac, racing through North Tunnel traffic, sideswiping vehicles as it raced for New Jersey.

"We got a live one," he said. "Get a crew ready!"

But I was on the phone already, calling it in. I could see the Caddy on one of my monitors now, doing seventy easy, weaving in and out of traffic. I was just hanging up the phone when George's voice came over the walkie-talkie.

"Breaker breaker, we got a smoker!" he said. "Caddy went by doin' eighty, easy! And there's a caravan of flat-beds ahead, takin' their time. . . . God *knows* what they're haulin'. . . ."

On another monitor, the Caddy was sideswiping another car, then careening against the tunnel wall, hitting the guard-rail, and rocketing on.

"We're on it, George," I told him, but we really weren't, were we?

CAPTAIN ALEXANDER LANGE, NYFD

Though this was not an instance of arson, the same investigative techniques pertain, and our reconstruction of the tragedy in the Manhattan Tunnel has been confirmed by every other local and federal agency involved. I must caution you that in granting this interview, I am speaking as a private citizen and not as a representative of the New York City Fire Department. I do appreciate your confidence in my opinion.

The runaway vehicle, the Cadillac driven by Billy Watson, which we estimate was traveling at ninety miles per hour, came upon a stopped vehicle, a taxi driven by Gholam Shivakumar. Mr. Shivakumar's vehicle had experienced a blow-out, and in response to this, Mr. Shivakumar applied his brakes, coming to a sudden stop.

Mr. Watson swerved to avoid rear-ending the stopped taxi and ran up on the elevated sidewalk alongside the tunnel, which, in concert with Mr. Watson's extreme speed, served as a sort of ramp, essentially launching the Cadillac into the air.

Dennis Correll, tunnel and bridge agent with the Tri-State Transit Authority, was at his post in the final guard booth at the New Jersey end of the tunnel. He apparently saw the oncoming vehicle as it flew toward him, and ducked, just before the top of the guard booth was sheared away.

Unfortunately for Agent Correll, his quick reflexes were not enough to save his life, or that of anyone within a reasonably close proximity, because the Cadillac met its final destination by way of the third of three flatbed trucks that we now know were convoying canisters of highly volatile hazardous waste materials for the purpose of illegal disposal.

Specifically, Mr. Watson's Cadillac struck the rear of the third truck. The resultant explosion was simultaneous with the third truck ramming the second truck, the cargo of which also erupted explosively, and the second truck into the first, with the same explosive result. The three explosions were right on top of each other, like one cannonball after another.

These interrelated explosions took place at what is commonly called the Jersey Curve of the tunnel, a point at which traffic jams are the norm. That evening was no exception. The trucks, even as they were exploding, collided devastatingly with these backed-up vehicles, and cars began piling up one on top of the other.

The best that can be said for the victims is that they died quickly.

It's difficult to convey the heat, and the force, involved

here. To give you an idea, the "Welcome to New Jersey" sign *melted*. And, of course, the New Jersey end of the tunnel caved in.

This cave-in created another problem. The explosions had stopped, but their fiery aftermath remained. In fact, a sort of firestorm had been created, and to explain its size, and its power, I might best compare it to a hurricane—a hurricane of fire. With its forward progress to New Jersey obstructed, it whipped in upon itself and, essentially, headed back to Manhattan, where the open air of the tunnel summoned it for further feeding, further fueling. . . .

In nanoseconds, the explosion sucked up every molecule of air, creating a fierce vacuum. The nearby limousine hired by Carl Weinstein of Weinstein Apparel, Inc., immediately imploded—in what you might describe as an accordion effect—instantly killing Weinstein and his passenger, Bambi Benson, as well as his driver, Rick Johnson.

Now our full-fledged firestorm, trailing a comet's tail of plasma, moved down the tunnel. The next vehicle it encountered was a camper owned by the late Jack Feeney (his wife, Jane, and seven-year-old daughter, Brenda, were also victims) and the thousand-degree shock wave took the camper's shell off the vehicle as easily as a hat taken by the wind.

The camper shell, flipping, melting, crashed through the windshield of the late Sylvia Silverstein, a Teaneck, New Jersey, housewife in a Ford Taurus. According to our reconstruction of the chronology of the disaster, Mrs. Silverstein had apparently been tailgating the camper. However, there is no reason to think if Mrs. Silverstein had maintained a proper distance from the camper that the result would have been any different.

For your purposes, I suppose, a complete listing of the victims who found themselves in the firestorm's path would be unwieldy. Suffice to say, each car it passed ignited as if doused in gasoline; again, the only blessing is the speed with which heat like this would end one's life. The end for these innocent bystanders came so quickly, the horror of their death did not, in most cases, have time to register, thankfully.

At midriver there is, of course, a passage between the north and south tubes of the tunnel; above is a building, a ventilation tower. The double doors of the midriver passage were not airtight—no reason for them to be, really—or at least until this happenstance no one ever saw any reason.

At any rate, as the firestorm rounded the curve toward Manhattan, it ''sensed'' the airflow of the passageway behind those double doors, and the firestorm forked, part of it maintaining its journey down the tunnel, a branch of it blasting through those midriver corridor doors and ripping them off their hinges.

The resultant shock waves caved in the corridor beyond, a corridor that could, of course, have provided a passageway for any survivors to make their way to the South Tunnel.

And, twenty stories above, a painting crew—I'm afraid I don't seem to have their names in my notes, but there were four of them, of ages ranging from twenty-two to thirty-eight, if I recall—was giving the trim of the midriver building's glass dome a fresh coat of paint. Up on their scaffolding, they would have had no time to escape it, even if they'd seen it coming, the explosion ripping up the ventilation shaft beneath them.

Did you get the diagram I provided? The airflow in those ventilation towers is controlled by massive iron louvers, but despite their thickness, in that incredible heat, the louvers twisted as if made of wax as a virtual tongue of flame licked ever upward.

The explosion jettisoned the painting crew through the glass dome and sent them tumbling into the night like human embers from a Roman candle.

I hope these attempts at description are not in bad taste; normally, I try to stay as detached and scientific as possible, in making a report, but this was unusual, and of course I'm not speaking in an official capacity. But let me tell you— bystanders on either side of the river reported that the mid-river tower resembled nothing so much as an erupting volcano.

ASHLEY CRIGHTON

Did I mention we had a sunroof? Well, we had a sunroof on the car, and normally I wouldn't open it up, in cold weather, but I was getting some great shots of the tunnel on my 8mm. It was eerie down there—the curved brick walls had a greenish glow, like the Emerald City of Oz, only I wasn't sure why. Were the bricks green? The horizontal row of lights, on left and right, hugging the ceiling, seemed to be emitting more of an off-white light, not green.

Anyway, I was getting some great shots, and I didn't even notice the heat, I was so into it.

I just suddenly felt somebody grab my legs—turned out to be Mom—and yank me down inside, and then, Jesus! Excuse me, but even just thinking back, I can't believe what I saw, it was like a comet tore across the car, and the heat was like a million sunlamps.

Mom had seen the fire coming before Dad did, just half a second before him, but *before* him, because otherwise I would have been in deep trouble. I'd be dead, is what I'd be.

Because if I'd been up there when he threw the brakes on, I bet I would have been thrown right out of the car and into that oncoming comet of fire. You see me shake? I'm shaking just thinking about it. . . .

The intense heat made every window in the car break, not break exactly, and shatter isn't the word—more like spiderweb, and through the spiderwebby windows we could see all sorts of shades of yellow and orange and blue, all around us, and it was like being a muffin in the oven, only that makes it sound too nice.

LATONYA WASHINGTON

I didn't see no fireball comin', I be sittin' starin' out the window, my head all full of Nordell, worryin' he be missin' me, at two they ain't no baby, you know, they know when mama ain't around.

So when that white driver, he throw on the brakes all a sudden, I don't see it comin'. The bus smash up against that sidewalk and rail, and us four, we go sailin', and so do that guard, the one that give Kadeem all that shit? Kadeem, he don't have to worry about gettin' even with that guard no more, 'cause that guard, he go flyin' like Superman, right into the windshield, like somebody shot out of a gun and he goes smack like a bug. Only this big bug hit the *inside* of a windshield.

Somebody say, "Holy shit," and don't you think that's about the worse thing you can hear somebody say at a time like that, and I look around and this big old fireball come barrelin' down the tunnel at us, like somethin' in a damn movie.

Like a fist of fire, it smack us and roll over us, and we roll, too, the bus on its side goin' over and over and over, and shake us up inside of there like Chiclets in a box. We roll over some car, I seen it later, we smash it flat like a beer can under your heel, but rollin' over that car made the bus flip kind of sideways and the bus nose got up on the rail of that sidewalk, and go flyin' forward, and all around us, damn! *Fire!* Orange and yellow and blue! We was *inside* it! I never seen nothin' so beautiful or so ugly, and hot? Shit! Crawl inside a damn oven and maybe you get a little idea.

So the bus is skiddin' along, tearin' hell out of that rail, screechin' like fingernails on a blackboard, till finally it come to a stop, nose on the rail, and that fire move on by us. Goin' lookin' for new meat, I guess.

That white driver, he be slump over the wheel, out cold.

Four of us, we kind of try to get straight with the world, only the world be tipped some. Mikey, that little crackhead, he go and cry in a corner, like a baby. He was a bigger baby than Nordell. Kadeem, he kick at that lock cage 'tween us and the driver. Only big as he was, Kadeem couldn't kick it loose.

We stuck in there. Fire's gone, but still hot, lots of smoke, and sparks from up above be fallin' like orange rain outside the windows.

What's *that* about? I wonder.

MADELYNE THOMPSON

There's no way to describe it. That stupid parody of "New York, New York" I was singing caught in my throat when I saw that ball of fire coming.

I ducked, hit the floor, and then fire was all around me, though I couldn't see it, I was covering my head with my arms, my face to the floor, but I could hear it, it was like a ghostly roar, and I heard my tires explode and the car dropped hard on its axle and then my windows exploded and glass rained all over me.

And the goddamn car stereo kept playing *La Traviata.*

First thing I did was turn it off.

As the firestorm streaked toward the Manhattan Tunnel entrance, the rounded walls began to shake and crack; every patched-over or overlooked structural weakness became stressed beyond endurance. Steam conduits split their seams, shooting scalding jetstreams in every direction. Even that massive Art Deco statue of a woman, that was as familiar to residents and tourists alike as the Statue of Liberty herself, wasn't immune. It had been there since the late twenties or early thirties, I understand. She cracked in two. Fell apart.

That was part of when the entrance at the mouth of the tunnel caved in, sending tons of concrete and rebar and rubble raining down, crushing the cars below that had just entered.

But the mouth wasn't so blocked that the flames couldn't find their way out, and the firestorm found its way up the ramp out of the tunnel, pitting windshields of cars with heat-driven debris, causing cars to bump into each other like a damn demolition derby.

Sorry. Again, I apologize if I haven't stayed as detached as I should. You have my full permission to edit this in any manner you desire.

At any rate, approximately a million tons of infrastructure came avalanching down, closing off the tunnel completely, cutting off the firestorm, leaving a cloud of dust mingling with smoke at the now sealed-off tunnel entrance.

And it was over—the explosion that is. Because for the poor bastards—excuse me—trapped in that tunnel, it was really just beginning.

3

SYMPHONY OF DESPAIR

In the immediate aftermath of the explosion, through the clouds of dust and smoke, came a cacophony of screams and moans and cries for help. Outside the sealed-off tunnel entrance, several of the piled-up cars were aflame, and more than one person ran fleeing from a fiery vehicle, a human torch. Others were trapped within, their fragile human tissue caught within twisted metal coffins.

BARBARA SMALLEY, M.D.

Our driver, this Kit Latura, had just turned off Varick Street to pull into the tunnel when the world turned surreal—it was like a fiery arm was reaching out for us. He swerved, and our windows were suddenly pelted with red-hot debris!

Next thing I knew, he'd stopped and was out of the car

before I'd caught my breath. We were actually on the floor of the limo, Dr. Samuels and me, John and me, neither one of us wearing seat belts—what is it that makes people in limos think they're immune to the need for seat belts? John was sprawled on his back, like a tipped-over turtle, mouth open, eyes wide; it would have looked comical if I wasn't scared shitless myself.

I heard Latura say, "Mother of God," and then the door opened and he looked in at us; we were still on the floor. His eyes were tight.

"Doctors," he said, "you got work to do."

He was right. It was like a goddamn war zone. No matter how many hours you might've logged in the ER, nothing could prepare any doctor for this, short of a battlefield stint.

I was barely out of the car when I saw a man engulfed in flames, screaming, running—the worst thing he could do, feeding the flames.

But Latura was on him in a heartbeat, tackling him to the ground, stripping off his black jacket and smothering the flames, telling him, "You're gonna be okay! You're gonna be fine!"

John moved in to see what he could do for the burn victim, when a young woman, her dress torn and bloody, staggered up to Latura.

VICKI HENDERSON

I could barely talk. I felt like I was in a dream, I mean nightmare. I was crying when I asked him, I don't even know how he could understand me; but I said, think I said, "My father . . . please help my father. . . ."

And I grabbed his hand and tugged him over to that rubble heap where the tunnel entrance used to be. The fancy statue of a lady that was over the entry had fallen and a large slab of it had crushed our car. The rider's side wasn't so bad and I had managed to crawl out. But my dad was in the front seat, oh God, it was crumpled like a paper cup, and Daddy was trapped in there, and his heart is bad anyway, I was so afraid for him, his face was all smudged with soot or dirt or something and it was all contorted, he was in terrible pain. The door on his side was blocked shut by another chunk of the broken lady.

This man, this Mr. Latura, pulled the concrete away and yanked the door open; he had amazing strength in his arms. It was like something in a Hercules movie.

Daddy was moaning. "My legs . . . my legs . . ."

I was losing it. "Please help him! You've got to help him!"

But Mr. Latura was calm. It was like he was trying to help us be calm by keeping his cool. He said to Daddy, gentle but firm, "I'm going to move you on the count of three. Try to help out, okay? Ready? One . . . two . . . *three*!"

Daddy started to scream and I covered my ears as Mr. Latura lifted him down onto the pavement.

"Oh, God," I said, covering my mouth.

Daddy's right leg was all mangled and bloody; you could see the muscle. And bone. It was awful.

Mr. Latura moved quickly and with authority that made me feel better. He stripped off his necktie and looped it around Daddy's thigh. Then he got a silver pen out of his pocket, one of those expensive Mark Cross ones? And he twisted the knot and sort of ratcheted the tension, to stem the bleeding.

Then he said to me, casual as if saying "pass the salt": "Here—hold this for me."

Meaning the pen, where it was twisted in the tie.

"Can you do that?" he asked. "Can you hold this for me?"

I felt so much better. His voice was soothing. And it felt good to be helping. I nodded, taking charge of the makeshift tourniquet.

And then he went on to help somebody else.

OFFICER JIM DOHERTY, NYPD

We were the first sector car to get there, my partner Chuck Bradley and me, but the sirens said more help was coming, and soon. That was a relief, because in five years, I never saw anything like this. Wrecked cars, wrecked people, scattered to hell and gone. Blood. Rubble. Smoke. Shit!

I tell you, I thought this guy Latura was some EMS chief who got there ahead of us. He seemed to be in charge, and he was in a white shirt and dark pants and, hell, what can I say? I thought he was in charge!

He sure *took* charge, pointing over to some of the less-injured victims who were milling about among the wrecked cars and the debris.

"Get these people away from here!" he said to us. "Get 'em over by the curb, now!"

I didn't argue with him. Chuck and me started guiding these people over to the curb, one at a time, and Latura and a couple of doctors, who, as it turns out, just happened to be on the scene, were doing a damn good job, under the circumstances, you know, considering.

And before long, an ambulance screamed in, and EMS guys, real ones, and more beat cops, and the whole battery of First Response teams, fire, cops, the Jaws of Life crew.

But you know what? For the longest damn time, this Latura stayed in charge. And it turns out he's a damn limo driver!

BARBARA SMALLEY, M.D.

John and I were doing our best with the injured, and before long, we were as bloody as the worst of them. But I was proud of John. He really was a hell of a doctor.

But I was more impressed with Latura.

After the Emergency Medical Service vehicles rolled in, things let up a little, but John and I stayed at it—Latura, too. He waved me over.

"What?" I asked.

He said, "I got a second-degree burn over here! Guy in the Mets jacket's a bilateral tension pneumo. Find somebody with a needle."

"What the hell kind of limo driver *are* you?"

"Pays to speak a lot of languages in a city this size."

I took care of his request, then caught up with him again when he called out for the Jaws of Life. That meant there was somebody alive trapped in the car under the rubble heap he was poking at.

It would take a while for the Jaws to get there, and from the sounds coming from that car, I figured somebody needed medical attention.

A woman within was moaning, crying, "Oh, God . . . oh my God, no! He can't be . . . somebody help him! Somebody help Roberto! Somebody help my husband!"

There were just enough spaces between chunks of rocks and rubble to see her, trapped inside the front seat, a young, pretty Hispanic woman next to her equally young but deceased husband. His eyes were wide open and she was, understandably, freaking out.

Latura was saying, "Look here. Look here! What's your name, darlin'?"

"Rose . . . Rose . . . Rosario."

She was slipping into shock.

He gently turned her head away from her dead husband.

"Rosario, this is Dr. Smalley. She's gonna stay with you, and everything's gonna be fine."

He turned to me, looking over my shoulder. "Here comes the Jaws. . . . Okay, Doc—you keep her talking. Don't let her look at him again."

And he left me in charge.

MICHAEL WELLER, EMS

My partner Lou Silverberg and me, we were the first EMS techs on the scene; we could see this civilian had taken charge, and were grateful, because at any accident scene or disaster site, it's helpful to have somebody who keeps his head and maybe has some medical and/or supervisory skills, who can minimize the problems and help avoid panic from setting in among the injured and other survivors; bystanders, too.

But now the first team was here, if you know what I mean, and it was better to have trained personnel in charge, you know, so I approached the guy and said, "Step back, sir— we'll take it from here."

Then the guy turns to me and I'll be damned if it isn't Kit Latura!

"Chief?" I said, kind of numbly.

He extended his hand and said, "It's Weller, right?"

I shook his hand and said, "Yes, sir."

He nodded toward a crushed car, where a woman was kneeling by the passenger window; later I learned this woman was a doctor. "There's a girl in there going into shock fast. Stick her with five cc's of ad, *now*."

Lou, who'd been on the job only six months or so, didn't know Latura and seemed confused or skeptical or something; but I nodded at him, conveying an order to do as Latura said, and Lou hustled off.

Black smoke was swirling, sirens wailing, the injured crying, moaning, those helping out offering reassurance in strong, commanding voices. It was a symphony of despair, and of hope; it's a familiar tune guys like us hear all the time, and never get used to. If I ever do, I'm quitting.

Latura was slowly scanning the area, seeing where he could help next.

I stood close to him and whispered, "You better get the hell out of here, before someone else recognizes you."

"Helping these people takes precedence over any concern I might have for—"

I put my hand on his shoulder. "Chief, we got it covered. See for yourself."

And we did have; a lot of help was on the scene now, not just our people, either—cops, fire department, everybody and his duck.

"What the hell happened?" Latura asked. "Terrorists? A bomb . . . ?"

"Apparently it's an accident. Word is, it's a midnight hauler, toxic waste dumper, that got rear-ended."

"Hell," Latura said softly. "That *is* a bomb."

"Yeah, well, nothing confirmed."

"What's the situation on the Jersey side?"

"Sealed shut, too. Fucking nightmare."

"We got people inside?"

I nodded. "Whether any of them are alive at this point, we don't know."

"Where's your chief?"

"Standing in front of me."

He liked hearing me say that; his smile was faint, but it spoke volumes.

"Your *new* chief," he corrected.

"California's answer to the East Coast's problems, you mean?"

Latura chuckled. "Yeah, him."

"Headed for the midriver passage in the South Tunnel."

Latura nodded; then he extended his hand again and we shook, and for a guy who holds it all in, he gave me a hell of a warm look.

"You better get back to work," he said.

And I did, and that was the last I saw of him.

ASHLEY CRIGHTON

The fire was gone, but there was plenty of smoke. It may seem funny, after a crash like that, that the first thing I'd do was climb up on the sunroof with my video camera and shoot more footage. But that's exactly what I did.

I wish I could say it was because I have the true instincts of a reporter, but that would be a lie.

Truth is, I don't remember doing it, but when we played the tape back, you could see, through the smoke in the tunnel, terrible images I'd captured, and sounds. Flames and wreckage everywhere, screams, cries of pain, somebody yelling, "Help me, somebody please, *help* me!"

A policeman was walking down that raised sidewalk toward us; he was a big black man and he was sort of jogging, using a walkie-talkie.

"Can anybody hear me?" he was saying into it. "We've got a fire burning toward the Jersey end, the ventilation doesn't seem to be pulling the smoke out. . . . Is anybody there?''

But the only answer his walkie-talkie gave him was a bunch of static.

All of that is on my tape and I don't remember it happening. What I first remember is that policeman—he said he was Officer Tyrell—jumping down from the sidewalk, climbing over its railing to help Daddy out of our crashed station wagon. Then Daddy helped Mom out.

For once I was glad Mom was a schoolteacher; she immediately became very efficent. Calm as a fire drill. She helped me down from the sunroof. I was having trouble seeing, my eyes were all watery, the smoke was awful. We were all coughing, me worst of all.

"Come on, baby," Mom said. "Come on—give me a hand."

Mom got our suitcases out and opened them and started taking clothes out, wetting them down, using a bottle of Evian water.

She handed me a wet blouse of mine. "Breathe through this, baby."

Mom handed Dad a wet shirt and then gave Officer Tyrell some other wet clothing, I don't know what exactly, maybe a T-shirt, but whatever it was, he put it over his nose as he moved on.

Oh, before he did that, he said, "You folks stay together. I'm going further up."

Dad said to me, "Don't worry, I'm sure help is on the way. Right, Officer?"

But Officer Tyrell didn't say anything; he was putting the wet whatever up on his face. Maybe he nodded. I'm not sure.

I mean, I'm trying to tell you what happened, but it's like trying to remember a dream. And even the most vivid dream you have trouble holding on to.

And nightmares, well it's only human to want to forget them.

ROGER TRILLING

The funny thing, funny strange that is, is that while our Mercedes looked as if it had been crushed by the world's largest trash compactor, neither Eleanor nor myself was more than mussed; neither of us had more than a scratch, either. The car, what was left of it, was on its side against the elevated sidewalk's guardrail, and we'd had to climb up and over and out.

Now we stood brushing ourselves off much as you might after stepping inside from a mild dusting of snow. In retrospect, we must have been in some sort of mild shock, but at the time I felt good about how calm we were taking this. Particularly Eleanor, who definitely had her high-strung moments.

A black police officer came trotting down the roadway toward us, appearing out of the smoke like a reassuring apparition.

"George Tyrell," he said, "Transit Authority. You folks okay?"

Eleanor was clinging to me, and my arms were around her. I squeezed her tight, so glad we were alive.

"We're fine . . . I think," I said. "Thank you for asking."

Then Eleanor pushed away from me, and I'll never forget the look of terror in her eyes as she started to say something, but it caught in her throat. She stepped away, and stared down the tunnel past the wall of smoke-streaming, fiery cars.

"Cooper," she said. "Where's Cooper? Oh, God—have we lost Cooper?"

The officer frowned and said, "Who's Cooper? Is he your son?"

He didn't know how close he'd come.

"Can you give me a description?" he asked.

Then Cooper answered with a mournful howl from far-away down the hellish corridor.

"We have to go to him!" Eleanor squealed, her voice mingling hope and fear.

"You folks stay right here," the officer said. "I'll round him up. Just stay put."

And, to her credit, Eleanor did; but I could understand how she felt. I loved Cooper, too, if not with the obsessiveness my wife did.

And hearing his lonely, eerie, echoing howl was unsettling indeed.

ROY NORD
(excerpts from cell-phone transcript)

Serena? Roy. God, I'm glad to get through to you; I've been hitting the damn redial button and getting nothing but static.

I'm afraid we ran into a little problem on the way to the airport. . . . It's already on the news? Any word of rescue efforts? . . . No, Jonno didn't make it. Neither did the HumVee. Thank God for seat belts, not that Jonno's did him any good, poor bastard.

Now, listen carefully—I want you to stand by the phone for my occasional, well, let's call them "broadcasts." I want you to tape-record my thoughts, which I'll share with you when I'm able. This will make an excellent chapter in the autobiography. . . . Frightened? Hell no! I thrive on challenges.

Recording? Good.

I'm here in the tunnel next to my Hummer; its nose is smashed against a blackened tile wall. From where I stand, I can't see any flames, but you can hear them, crackling. The smoke is a constant, but the ventilation must be working somewhat, because it's not suffocating.

My friend, my good right arm, Jonno, sustained a fatal head wound when my HumVee smashed into the wall. I covered his poor bleeding ruined head with my jacket, and a Hugo Boss suit was never sacrificed to a nobler cause. Then I extricated myself and got out to survey the situation, covering my nose and mouth with a bandanna.

As I was moving down the tunnel, strewn with the twisted, sometimes fiery wreckage of vehicles—stopping to check for survivors, and finding none—I finally encountered a Transit Authority cop, an Afro-American built like a fullback; he was a comforting sight.

"Goddamn," I told him, "it's good to see a uniform. What's the situation here?"

"I'm afraid I don't know any more than you do, sir—hey! Jesus! You're Roy Nord—the Territory Beyond guy!"

Even under these circumstances, I couldn't repress a grin. "Guilty as charged, Officer."

"I'm George Tyrell," he said, and we shook hands. Then he grinned back at me and added, "You know, I've got a pair of your shoes."

"Glad for the business. If you know the way out, I'll send you a free pair."

A good man, this Tyrell. He chuckled grimly and I walked along with him, back the way I'd come, toward Manhattan; he was charting us a course with a flashlight that cut through the drifting smoke like a single headlight.

He began checking the crashed vehicles for survivors.

"Don't bother," I said. "I've checked more pulses in the

47

last ten or fifteen minutes than a draft-board doctor.''

He sighed grimly. We continued along.

"You didn't answer my question," I said. "Is there a way out?"

He raised his eyebrows. "There is a passage to the South Tunnel, about half a mile up."

"Splendid!"

"Not really—it's collapsed. Blocked as hell. No passage, there."

"Mind if I take a look for myself?"

"You're wasting your time, Mr. Nord. I'm tellin' ya, there's no way through. . . ."

We were back here at the HumVee by then, and I told him, "That may well be true, George, but you see, one time a friend of mine and I lost our way, spelunking the Csardis Cave. My friend started to panic, saying, 'There's no way out, we're lost, we're hopelessly lost' . . . but you know what, George? I'm still here. Catch my drift?"

He caught it all right. He nodded and shrugged and went on his way.

The luckiest break I had, even though it was anything but lucky for poor Jonno, was crashing head-on. That meant my trunk was undamaged, and as you know, Serena, my gear bags were in there, ready for my Colorado trip.

Pays to be prepared—an old Eagle Scout like yours truly knows that, if anything. Stay at the phone, Serena, and keep your finger on the record button: I'll be back.

4

TUNNEL VISION

As a news helicopter circled overhead, its spotlight probing the chaos below, EMS trucks and various other rescue vehicles screeched into position, as cops put sawhorse barriers in place, cordoning off the area. NYPD officers and tunnel and bridge agents were guiding evacuating cars from the Manhattan-bound South tube of the tunnel, waving them into a single lane of traffic next to the elevated sidewalk. A wrecker was allowed through the cordon, and it headed down the other lane, into the tunnel.

More than one onlooker reported seeing a man fitting Kit Latura's description hopping onto the back fender of that wrecker, as it headed for the midriver passage.

Within the South Tunnel, bedlam reigned. Cars were inching forward, nudging fenders; but progress was so slow, the occupants of some cars were abandoning them in favor of the elevated sidewalk, where they ran pell-mell, occasionally colliding with uniformed Transit Authority officers running in the opposite direction. Some of those officers, spotting a driver in the process of abandoning a car, would force said driver back into his vehicle, even as a bullhorned voice advised the same thing: "Please stay in your cars and proceed out of the tunnel. You are in no danger."

The wrecker had to slow for cars passing abandoned vehicles, and if indeed Kit Latura had hitched a ride on the wrecker, he was witness to a disturbing array of images, images of panic, as a city faced one of its worst disasters.

FRANK KRAFT, DEPUTY CHIEF, EMS

Our Search and Rescue crew was probing the entrance to the midriver passageway, but gingerly, to say the least. The damn thing was totally collapsed. I was standing next to Chief Wilson—Dennis Wilson, like the Beach Boy; we used to make cracks about that behind the chief's back, frankly, because he was from California and had some attitudes that rubbed a native New Yorker the wrong way.

I don't mean to sound petty. I took some ribbing when Wilson was brought in, because I'd been with EMS for fifteen years, and at forty-five, I had five years on my new boss, easy. But I didn't mind. Hell, Latura was younger than me, too, and I never resented him for that.

It was Wilson's manner. Not cocky, but maybe a little too confident. You might say he took his grooming and management cues from Pat Riley, if that gives you an idea.

Anyway, we were assessing the possibilities, which I admit I thought were pretty goddamn grim. I'd just got off the walkie-talkie. You could hardly hear yourself think for all the shouts and bullhorn orders.

Wilson asked, "Any hope on the Jersey side?"

"Fifty-yard cave-in, minimum," I said. "Whatever's burning in there is as toxic as Trenton."

"Somebody needs to take a sample of that shit."

"Grace Lincoln says somebody already has."

Wilson nodded, and crossed to a crevice in the wreckage that was spilled onto the elevated sidewalk. He wore a throat-miked walkie-talkie, unlike my handheld. Some of our EMS guys, in full toxic gear, were feeding ropes into the worm-holelike opening.

Wilson leaned in. "Talk to me, Boom!"

From within the wormhole came the voice of Cathy Dix, an EMS tech with a specialty in explosives, which explained her black-humor nickname, Boom.

"Gimme a minute, Chief!" Boom called.

"If I had one," Wilson said tersely, "I would."

A familiar voice cut in: "Wanna buy some time?"

Familiar, but I couldn't believe I was hearing it.

"Jesus, Kit," I said, facing him. "What the hell are you doing here?"

"Just another citizen who picked the wrong evening to take the tunnel," he said. "And a whole hell of a lot luckier than some. . . . Frank, you've got to blow that tunnel shut. Seal it off!"

Wilson turned to face the man he replaced, and his expression couldn't have been colder. "You're not part of this, Latura. You're not authorized to be here. Leave—now."

Kit's expression was earnest; he didn't give Wilson any of the coldness back. In fact, he moved close to him and spoke somberly.

"Chief," he said, "please listen. We ran a terrorist hypothetical in ninety-three. The only fix for a fire in that tunnel is to blow the roof in and seal off the survivors from the fumes."

Wilson's smirk was disgusted. "Where I come from, Latura, you don't blow up a tunnel that's blown up already. Your input is noted, and appreciated. . . . Now move along.''

I said to Kit, ''The chief wants to go in here, through the midriver—''

Wilson got in my face. ''Don't you go justifying my actions to this criminal!''

Kit stepped between us, gently as he could, saying, ''We ran a simulation on the midriver, too. The victims'll all be dead, before you make it through.''

''A drill in ninety-three,'' Wilson said, glaring at Kit, ''is not reality. Today, *right now,* is reality. You may have run all sorts of drills, Mr. Latura, in your day, but at the moment you're not running a goddamned thing.''

''You're right,'' Kit said softly, even respectfully. ''I'm not. I'm just trying to help. Lives are at stake. Any differences any of us have had, in the past, need to be put aside.''

''I won't be lectured by you,'' Wilson said tightly. ''You offer me your help, well, I'll tell you how I value that offer. Every day on this job, I spend half my time trying to undo the damage you did to this department.''

Kit winced at that, then calmly said, ''Go through the midriver, they're dead before you get there. It's not an opinion. Check your computer.''

Wilson pointed a finger at Kit like a gun. ''You don't work here anymore. Get it?''

Heaving a disgusted sigh, Wilson moved back over to the wormhole.

I stood near Kit and said, almost whispered, ''You better take off, Kit. That son of a bitch will have you arrested.''

''You've got to convince him, Frank. He won't listen to me. But maybe he'll take it from you, you've got seniority, if not rank, over him. Get him to blow that tunnel shut.''

I shrugged in frustration. ''Kit, it's his show.''

Suddenly he was clutching my shoulder. ''It's nobody's

'show,' Frank. Hundred yards north, it's a funeral. A mass funeral. You think *I* caused the department some bad publicity? Let's see Chief Wilson dig out from under that.''

And he let go of my shoulder, but held me with his gaze before nodding and taking off in a sprint.

Then he was heading further into the tunnel, toward New Jersey.

"Kit," I said. "Goddammit, Kit. You found a way to make your situation worse, didn't you? Only you could do that. . . ."

I watched him go as he jogged uptunnel, bobbing and weaving amid the hundreds filing out in a mass exodus, obeying the bullhorn direction: "Lock your cars and proceed calmly out of the tunnel. You are not in any danger."

Then Kit disappeared into the evacuation as Wilson called out to me, "How 'bout a hand here?"

I lent him one, hauling Boom out of the passage. A tough, wiry little demolition expert, Boom actually was kind of cute, though right now you'd never guess it, smudged with dirt as she was, coughing, spitting.

"Sorry, Chief," she said to Wilson. "It's blocked solid."

"How far in?"

"Twelve feet. Structure's so shaky I wouldn't risk a firecracker, let alone any plastic."

"This doesn't sound like you, Boom," he said. "If anybody likes to make a noise, it's you. . . ."

"Not this time, Chief. Can't be done."

A frown creased his face. "I don't like that attitude."

She raised both palms. "It's not an attitude, Chief. It *can't* be done!"

Wilson's laugh was smug. "The person who says it can't be done is always interrupted by the person who just did it."

And our chief grabbed a helmet from one of the guys, and

snapped a rope to his harness and crawled inside.

"Help him along, boys," I said, and they started feeding the ropes in.

And, you know, the ropes kept sliding in, and before long, Boom looked at me and shrugged; he'd already made it in deeper than twelve feet.

His voice echoed out to us: "Here's a way! I can see a way!"

He started to say something else, but I honestly can't say, or even hazard a guess, as to what it might have been, because that was when a horrible grinding sound within the wormhole was followed suddenly by a horrendous crash of stone, steel, and rubble. Not a cave-in, exactly, just a shifting of the pickup sticks within, punctuated by a whoosh of dust blasting out through the hole, making all of us back up.

And that's how the chief died, and I assumed command.

LATONYA WASHINGTON

We be rattlin' that cage, Kadeem kickin' at it and shit, and that driver, I thought maybe he dead, seat-belt strap keepin' him in his seat, hangin' at a damn angle. But we must of woke him with the racket we make, he come to, see his friend the dead splattered guard, and look back at us, we grabbin' the cage, shoutin' at him.

"Hey, mister," I yell. "You gotta help us!"

He don't say nothin', he just unstrap his self and kind of keep his balance leanin' on the steerin' wheel, and pop open that door, make a kind of wheeze sound openin', crash didn't hurt it none.

But when he open it, the dead guard, he go tumblin' out, first one off the bus, and at the angle the bus is, nose up on the guardrail, it's maybe five foot. Sound like a big slab of meat hittin' concrete.

"Mister," I yell, "you can't just leave us here, man!"

"Watch me," he say.

Vincent say, "We got rights! You suppose to escort us!"

But that white driver, he don't give a shit. Not even when Kadeem grab that wire cage and shake it like a cat shakin' a rat it catch.

"You better pray I don't get out," Kadeem say, "'cause your ass is mine! You a dead man. A dead man!"

The driver say screw you or somethin' like that and drop out the door, on top of his dead friend, and lose his balance.

We go apeshit, runnin' toward the window, poundin' and hollerin' and jumpin' up and down, and I guess the weight must of shift or somethin', 'cause all a sudden the nose of the bus jump off that handrail where it be sittin', and the bus, it tip over on its side and hit the pavement, *slam!*

That white driver, he ain't got his balance yet, when the bus fall. He be under there. Get squished like a roach under a shoe. Didn't even have time to holler.

"You mus' be psychic," Vincent says to Kadeem. "He *is* a dead man."

A bright orange flash catch my eye, and I look up through the windows by the seats—bus be on its side, remember?—and I see somethin' real bad.

The tunnel, its ceiling be rip open and all sort of electrical line and cable and what you call it, conduit and stuff? They all tangle up and hangin' down, like the insides of some animal that got its gut rip open.

And it be sparkin', showerin' orange and yellow and white sparks on us like the damn Fourth of July, only this ain't no holiday.

ROY NORD
(excerpt from cell-phone transcript)

Okay, Serena. Recording again.

I've been on a stroll through purgatory. Loaded down with ropes, harness, and climbing gear now, suit coat and tie abandoned as mere accoutrements of civilization, I'm ready for the adventure ahead. But my adrenaline rush is tempered by the tragedy around me.

Even for a man of my experience, these sights and sounds are daunting: within my sight, a toxic fire is raging from roadbed to ceiling, flames licking up with unabated fury around the mangled frames of trucks and cars. From their positioning, I would hazard a guess that these trucks, flatbeds (though its difficult to tell *what* they were, quite frankly), may well have instigated the accident.

These vehicles have become one twisted mass of metal, their charred, fiery shells commingling in a grotesque work of modern sculpture. No one down here, in this section, this close to the explosion, could be left alive.

I have spotted what must be the midriver passage; the debris, the rubble, concrete, steel has spilled over the elevated sidewalk onto the roadbed like feed from a split grain sack.

Keep recording, Serena . . . this'll just take a few moments. . . .

Okay. Okay. I've made my way up the pile of rubble and I'm having a look inside the collapsed tunnel. There do seem to be some openings, some possibilities for passage. I'm going to carefully take a look inside.

You'll be hearing from me.

I tried the handle on the door on the driver's side of my car and it opened as if I were stepping out at the curb, in front of some SoHo shop. But the car I was stepping from was a blackened hulk, and the world around me a hellish chaotic nightmare—cars scattered like a spoiled child's discarded toys, smoldering, their drivers, their passengers, charred or crushed or both.

Shaken but not injured, I was immediately seized by a racking coughing jag, as an oily black haze billowed about me. It seemed a little clearer up ahead, maybe there was *some* ventilation going, and I got myself under control, the coughing fit easing up.

Was everybody dead but me?

As if in answer, pounding and yelling came echoing up the tunnel; fifty yards ahead, a small school-bus-type vehicle was on its side—and the sounds were coming from it. There *were* other survivors. . . .

But there wouldn't be for long, not with that sparking flash above the bus, as hot copper filings rained down on the bus, as if some fiendish crew of arc welders were at work up there.

I moved quickly toward the bus, slowly scanning the perimeter for any other sign of life or help, seeing nothing. But through the spiderwebbed windshield of the Department of Corrections bus, I could see four more survivors, teenagers, street kids who were screaming for help.

Their screams caught in their throats as they saw me, too.

I moved as close to the windshield as I dared. The rain of sparks nearby had me shaking, but I tried to keep it out of my voice as I called, "I'll try to find help!"

A dark, good-looking kid said, "Lady, you *are* help!"

"No," I said, "I need to find somebody in charge...."

"In charge of *what*?" a black girl said. She was maybe fourteen, fifteen, with hard cold eyes that were far older. "You got to help us, now!"

She was right.

That windshield was halfway broken in already; it was my only reasonable port of entry. Was there something I could use to bust it the rest of the way in? I looked around. A scorched suitcase lay amidst other, less promising rubble in the roadway. With its hard shell, it might just do the trick....

But when I went to pick it up by its handle, shit! The damn thing was as hot as a glowing coal!

Pulling down the sleeves of my coat over my hands, I managed to grip it and carted it over to the bus and used it as a bludgeon on the windshield, smashing out the already webbed glass, which disintegrated into little safety-glass pellets.

I was breathing hard, and it was just smoky enough to turn my breathing into another coughing jag, and just as I was trying to get myself together, wondering if the opening I'd made was large enough, an electrical hissing above me signaled a shower of sparks over my head, like a fairy was dusting my hair with stardust.

A sadistic fairy.

I covered my eyes with a hand, as if shielding my gaze from a bright sun, and risked a glance up and saw a cable jerking down out of the ceiling, plunging toward me like a thick black tree snake, well suited to that continuing hiss, and I dove into the bus, that deadly cable whipping right by where my head had been a moment ago.

Scrambling, I tried to get to my feet; in the sideways bus, I had landed at the bottom of steps and was in the mouth of the retracted door, an exit that could not be used because it led only to pavement . . . only my footing told me I wasn't standing on pavement, what *was* I standing on . . . ?

I looked down and saw my running shoes had found purchase on the lifeless legs of some poor squashed bastard the bus had fallen on!

Maybe I screamed, because I heard the girl saying, "I think she just meet our driver."

Clambering up in the sideways front of the bus, I was able to wedge my feet between the retracted door and the dashboard. Sparks—orange, yellow, white—continued to rain down on the bus, and that black hissing electrical snake was dangling, whipping around on its own energy.

"The keys, girl!" a big tall lean black kid said. "In the 'nition!"

"Key to this damn cage be on there!" the black girl shouted.

The keys were indeed in the ignition, and I plucked them out, and rustled through them, picking out a key that had a nonautomotive look and trying it on the cage's deadbolt. It worked, snapping back the lock.

Must have been my lucky day.

The big tall black guy shoved the others out of the way and was the first one out, climbing through the frame of the windshield and making an athletic leap from the nose of the bus, a feat that was as bold as his shoving to the head of the line had been gutless. He only narrowly missed the sparking cable that jiggled four feet from the metal of the bus hood.

"Run, O.J., run!" the black girl called derisively.

I helped the handsome kid climb up and over and through the broken-out windshield, and he nimbly timed his exit past the swinging, spark-spitting cable.

"Next!" I called.

But one kid, a smaller, younger one, was cowering in a corner, shivering as if he were freezing to death.

"Boy pick a bad time for a crack attack," the black girl said. "Mise well leave him."

"We can't do that," I said. "He's just a child. . . ."

Something passed across the cold eyes in the girl's dark face, something that melted them.

But then the coldness returned and the girl said, "You help yourself, lady! Me, I haulin' ass outta here—"

I grabbed her by the arm. Looking back, I don't know how I had the nerve; this kid was tougher than I'd ever be. On the other hand, I had just risked my life crawling in here to help her and her friends.

"We're not leaving him in here," I said tightly.

The black girl frowned, and got an indignant expression going; but she didn't say anything, and she didn't try to leave.

To the cowering kid, I said, "What's your name?"

"Muh-muh-Mikey."

"I'm Madelyne. I'm pretty scared. You scared, Mikey?"

"Real-real-really scared."

"Me, too. Me, too. I'd feel better with you at my side."

Mikey, still cowering, shook his head no.

Suddenly the black girl was right in his face. "Yo, Mikey! We *all* scared! Now get your skinny crack-suckin' ass out the window!"

Mikey swallowed and got to his feet.

I looked at the girl with admiration; she smiled a little, and I knew we were a team now.

"Sometime," she said, "you got to be firm with a chile."

"Go on," I told her. "Get on out of here. . . ."

"Name's Latonya Washington."

"You go on, Latonya. I'll take care of Mikey."

And Latonya climbed out the window, timed her jump past the swaying sparking cable, and Mikey and I were alone.

LATONYA WASHINGTON

This big cop, a brother with name tag say TYRELL, come up and herd me and Vincent and Kadeem away from the bus. Make us get far away as we could, but we could still see it, and so could he.

"Shit," he say.

We see what he could see, now. Under the bus, liquid be poolin' up, and it ain't water. The gas tank must of got ruptured. So there's the bus, in a pool of gasoline, and there's that cable dancin' and sparkin'. I see Madelyne in there inside, movin' with Mikey, and I start to holler, but didn't do no good. Them electrical guts hangin' down, sparkin', was noisy, like a hundred electric chairs fryin' a hundred poor killers.

This cop, this brother, Tyrell, he go closer and yell, "Lady! There's gas! Get outta there!"

But she must not of heard him.

Then that damn cable, like a big old snake with a life of his self, go jerkin' out of the ceiling, drop a couple feet closer to the metal of that bus hood.

Even without the gas, they be runnin' out of time.

Then the cop, Tyrell, took off full tilt up the tunnel. What was he doin', runnin' out on 'em?

MADELYNE THOMPSON

That cable was out there, swinging out of control, hanging farther down now, no more than a foot from the metal of the hood.

And I had Mikey up by the busted-out windshield, ready

to guide him out of there, when the damn cable seemed to spring at us like a fucking cobra, spitting sparks, not venom, nearly zapping us.

We jumped back.

Mikey said, "I don't wanna fuh-fuh-fry!"

"You're not going to fry, Mikey," I assured him, but you know what? I wasn't so sure.

I tried to think. In the case of lightning, what do you do? Don't get under a tree. Get back in your car because of the tires. The rubber tires. And I thought of my running shoes and their rubber soles. . . .

I wrestled out of my running shoes and slipped them on my hands, like ungainly mittens. Mikey's expression of wide-eyed terror turned puzzled.

"Are you kuh-kuh-razy? What're you . . . what're you . . . ?"

"I'm gonna grab that snake out there, Mikey, and when you see an opening, take it!"

And straddling the door and the windshield frame, I timed my move—and reached out, and pincered that damn cable with the rubber-sneaker soles, not six inches away from electrocution contact.

The cable resented my resourcefulness, and fought back, yanking me out of the bus, slamming me onto the hood, and as I tumbled off, and down, I managed two things: I landed on my feet, and I never let loose of my rubber-sole grip on that cable, I kept the son of a bitch clinched and held out at arm's length. . . .

That was when I smelled the gasoline.

And knew I was standing in it, in a pool of it.

Mikey was in the window and his eyes were wide and afraid and I yelled, "Mikey, move! Now!"

And Mikey moved—scrambled out of the windshield frame and onto the hood.

"Okay, Mikey—slide down easy . . . don't splash! Don't make waves, Mikey . . . nice and easy. . . ."

Like a child on a slide in the park, he eased down the bus into the gas and made only the tiniest splash while I wrestled my spitting black snake.

"Don't run till you're out on dry ground! Go! *Go!*"

And he went, running off to where the others stood, leaving me alone.

In a pool of gasoline.

Clutching a spark-spewing power line in my Adidas-shod hands.

5

POWER PLAY

An open area alongside the New Jersey River Building along the banks of the Hudson River became headquarters for the rescue operation, with representatives from Emergency Medical Services, New Jersey State Police, and tunnel and bridge agents of the Tri-State Transit Authority moving in and out of the base camp. A triage tent was in place, and another smaller tent provided an impromptu press room, as mobile news units from Live at Five *and all the networks vied for space.*

Within the New Jersey River Building itself, in the cramped control room, Norman Bassett and Grace Lincoln fought to create order in an atmosphere of highly charged chaos.

You couldn't hear yourself think. Everybody was talking on top of each other, phones were ringing off the hook. Norm and me, we were glued to our monitors. The South Tunnel monitors showed complete evacuation had been achieved, save of course for our people; weird seeing all those cars there, abandoned, doors yawning open. Like the end of the world. Like a plague hit, or a nuclear bomb.

Many of the North Tunnel monitors were dead, but a few showed hazy images, sometimes of people moving around. So we knew we had some survivors in there, and we knew we had a problem with all that damn smoke.

"Grace," Norm said, "get those other fans on!"

"They *are* on! Exhaust ducts must be blocked." I checked on it, threw some switches, and didn't like the result at all. "Goddamn! Number three just overloaded."

"Christ. How's their air?"

"Bad. Getting worse."

Then Norm got called over to the phone, and I kept working on the monitors, trying to sharpen up the images, but as smoky as the tunnel was, it was tough to tell what you had.

Then, suddenly, a very familiar figure appeared on one of the screens, looking right up at the camera, gesturing wildly.

"George," I gasped. "God, it's *George. . . .*"

My eyes started to tear up—I wasn't sure till that moment he was still alive—but I didn't give in to the emotion. George wouldn't let me: his gestures were so emphatic, conveyed so much urgency, I got immediately caught up in trying to decipher the meaning of this crucial game of charades he was playing.

He was making a scissors pantomime.

"Norm," I called, "I got George on the monitor! He's trying to—"

"I'm on conference call," Norm said in a harsh whisper, covering the mouthpiece, "with all three governors—handle it yourself."

My eyes were still on George. The scissors motion, then he'd raise his fist in the old power-to-the-people way.

"What are you trying to tell me, baby?" I whispered.

He kept repeating it—scissors, power-to-the-people—finally I panned the camera around to see what he might be referring to, and I could make out a bus, school-bus sort of vehicle, on its side, and above it a live electrical cable was dangling, shooting sparks. No people visible, just the bus, and the sparking cable . . .

I panned back to George and he was still making with the cutting gesture, and the upraised power fist and—

"Cut the power!" I shouted. I wheeled around in my chair and Norm was still glued to the phone, doing a lot more listening than talking, but when I said, "We gotta cut the power!" he just looked at me crossly and waved me off.

"Governor," Norm said, "we're doing all we can, but the situation isn't yet in hand. What do you want me to say? I can't stave off the media indefinitely. . . . I'm not comfortable, Governor, a misrepresentation like that could come back to haunt me. . . ."

I panned the camera back and saw something I'll never forget: a woman standing in a pool of gasoline leaked from the nearby toppled bus, and she was struggling with a power line gripped in hands protected by rubber-soled sneakers.

My heart jumped into my throat; I reached out and grabbed Norm's shoulder. "Norm, we gotta cut the power!"

But Norm was talking to the governor, or governors, not seeing any of this, and I didn't have clearance to make that level decision, you know, and I'm trying to get the courage to do it anyway when somebody's suddenly in our cubbyhole with us, taking the phone out of Norm's hand.

"He'll call you back," the guy says, and I'll be damned if it wasn't Kit Latura himself, hanging up the phone, while Norm looks up at him astounded as hell, more surprised than irritated.

"Good to see you, Chief," I said, a relieved grin flicking onto my face.

"What's the extension, Grace?"

"Who the hell are you?" Norm sputtered. "What gives you the right—"

"Latura," he said. "Used to work Emergency Rescue."

"Extension eight-zero-five," I told Latura, and while Norm looked on with glazed outrage Latura dialed the phone, waited for the ring, then held it out to Norm.

"You cut the power right now," Latura said, pointing to the monitor where the figure of the woman wrestled the spitting power cable, "or that woman's dead."

"Norm, listen to him," I said. "He's right. He's the former chief of Emergency Rescue; he knows what he's saying!"

Norm swallowed, twitched a frown—but with his eyes on the monitor where that woman was doing a dance with life and death, he took the phone, God bless him.

LATONYA WASHINGTON

Standin' back away from there, I feel helpess as Nordell, watchin' that brave white woman strugglin' to hold on to that buckin' cable.

Kadeem, he behind me, shakin' his head. "She's toast, man."

"Shut up," I say, and then I call out to her: "Drop that sucker! Drop it an' run! Come on, Madelyne—you can do it, girl!"

Then it was like the cable hear me cheerin' for the wrong side. It jerk her around like God in a bad mood was whippin' it, and I could tell she couldn't hole up under this much longer. Even from where we stood, you could see it in her face. She be makin' up her mind. She gone to go for it.

With all her might, she hurl that cable up in the air and take off runnin'.

Man, was that cable pissed off! Spittin' sparks, snappin' in the air, crackin' itself like a whip.

Me and Mikey, we screamin', sort of somewhere in between cheerin' her on and freakin' out. Vincent and Kadeem, they keepin' their cool, that macho bullshit, you know? But they be watchin', I think they kind of lookin' up to her. Maybe even rootin' for her. Madelyne, she one macho woman. She got the biggest balls in this damn tunnel.

Anyway, she runnin', feet still in the gas, the cable whippin', she slippin' but not fallin', cable fallin', and then she dive, flat out!

She in the air when that cable hit the puddle of gas, but somebody somewhere must of hit a big old breaker switch, cause' that cable stop its spittin' right fore it splashes in the gas. It lay there limp dick, hiss a little, but nothin' blow up.

Then we cheerin', Kadeem and Vincent, too, and Mikey and me rush over where Madelyne, she spread out on the concrete, and we help her up and shit.

Vincent, he come over, swaggerin' like, and say, "Now that's the kind of woman I been lookin' for."

She didn't pay him no mind. He could of picked a better time to come on to her.

I don't know if I ever saw a prettier sight than George with that big shit-eating grin looking up at the camera and out of that monitor at me, giving me the thumb-and-forefinger okay sign.

"She's okay!" I yelled.

A collective sigh of relief passed through the cramped control booth.

I looked up at Latura and mouthed a silent thanks, and he just nodded and smiled ever so slightly.

But then Norm was on his feet and in Latura's face. "I don't know whether to thank you or throw your ass out."

"You're welcome," Latura said.

"Just who the hell *are* you?"

"We met a couple years ago, at the interdepartmental conference in ninety-three. Remember the terrorist hypothetical? I headed that up."

Norm squinted, nodded, recalling. "Latura. I thought you were canned in ninety-four. When did you get back with EMS?"

"I didn't." He leaned in next to me, looked at the monitor; I'd panned the camera so I could see George gathering up the woman and a handful of kids.

"Carbon monoxide's climbing fast," I told him.

"Now just hold on!" Norm said, cutting between us. "If you're not back with EMS, who's given you authority to take command?"

"Nobody," Latura said calmly. "I just happened to be on the scene when the shit hit the fan. A concerned citizen with some expertise trying to help out, is all."

"Jesus!" Norm said. "You had no right—"

"To save that woman's life?" I interrupted. "Norm, he knows his stuff. He's willing to help. This is no time for protocol, or personalities."

"We got survivors to rescue," Latura said.

Norm had a constipated expression. He knew Latura and I were right, but he must have also been thinking about all the years he'd put in, and how he didn't need any stumbling blocks between now and retirement.

"If you're going to work with us," he said kind of lamely, "I'm going to need some sort of authori—"

"Please," Latura said disgustedly, and leaned in next to me again. "How's their air? Break it down."

"It's like the devil passed gas in there," I said. "We're exchanging at a rate of about a million cubic feet per hour—*one twentieth* the usual rate. . . ."

Latura turned to Norm. "Can you pull a schematic up on your computer?"

Norm said, "I've got better than that coming," and as if on cue, the doors burst open and a phalanx of our engineers came struggling through with a large, dusty wooden box that might have been a midget's coffin.

"Let's get these desks shoved together," Norm said, and Latura pitched right in with the rest of us as we bunched up the steel desks into one large table. No time to stand on ceremony: I swept the desktops clear with the side of my arm, in/out baskets, manila file folders, family photos, just so much junk on the floor now.

The engineers slammed the box down. It creaked with age and puffs of dust rose. Then they went at it with a crowbar and some heavy-duty screwdrivers. Norm hadn't said a word to me about this, and I was mystified as to its contents.

Soon they were answering my unasked question by popping the ancient, rusted locks, flipping back the lid.

"Careful," Norm said. "Careful . . ."

The lid got tossed on the floor with everything else, and the remaining four sides folded down, on hinges.

"Jesus," I said. My eyes must have been popping.

We were looking at a perfect scale model of the Manhattan Tunnel. Everything was there: New York, New Jersey, the Hudson River, the building we were standing in on the New Jersey side, the mouths of the tunnel, even the statue of that lady that had crashed and blocked the New York entry.

"The original architectural model," Norm explained to Latura. "When they glued this thing together, Woodrow Wilson was in the White House."

"Did you vote for him, Norm?" I asked.

Norm took that well, and everybody grinned; Latura's eyes locked with mine and he nodded, as if to say, Thanks for relieving the tension.

"So like the cop asked me this morning," Latura said, "where's the fire?"

Norm told the engineers to take the model apart; it was designed so that sections could be lifted off, but the guys had to be careful—this was a procedure that hadn't been done in sixty years or so.

Norm gestured at the delicately detailed innards of the model. "North tube, South tube, river, riverbed . . . the tunnels are rectangles set within each tube. Okay, guys—again . . ."

The top half of the North Tunnel was lifted off, and we were looking down at a horizontal section complete with tiny Model T Fords, even horse-drawn beer wagons, heading for a miniature New Jersey on a scale-model roadbed. It was cuter than a dollhouse, but a lot more instructive.

Norm was gesturing again. "Toxic fire and first collapse are right about here."

Now it was my turn to point, from a duct to the midriver

passage to a duct. "Blocked, blocked, and blocked," I said.

Latura pointed to a room on the south side of the tube connecting to a guard booth. "What's this?"

Norm shrugged. "I'm not sure. It's not labeled, is it? No. Well, a bunkhouse for the sandhogs, you suppose? I understand that when they built these tunnels, the lead guys could be down there as long as thirty-six hours. My understanding is there were little rooms dug out so they could catch naps between shifts."

Latura was frowning in thought. "You think the guardhouse connects?"

"I doubt it," Norm said. "There were renovations in seventy-two, you know. I would imagine those rooms got sealed off then. Not much good to us now."

Latura pointed to the midriver passage. "What about the connecting tunnel? Wilson give an estimate of when they'll get through?"

Norm called out to anyone who might have the answer: "Anybody get an estimation from Chief Wilson on when his team might break through at the midriver?"

The answer came from an unexpected source.

A male voice from the doorway said, "Not unless somebody's got a Ouija board."

In the doorway, his suit dusty, his face smudged, expression grim, Deputy Chief Frank Kraft leaned against the jamb as if exhausted.

"Another section of the midriver passage collapsed about twenty minutes ago," Kraft said glumly. "The chief is an apparent casualty."

Silence draped the room for a few moments, then Latura said, "Anybody else injured, or . . . ?"

"No. No, he went in alone. Grandstanding son of a bitch." Kraft shook his head. "Sorry. That was inappropriate, but goddammit, I don't like to see needless loss of life. Not on my watch."

And with Wilson gone, it *was* Kraft's watch, now.

"So," Latura said. "What are we looking at?"

Kraft sighed. "To safely clear that passageway? Seven hours, minimum. That's *if* the rest of the shaft doesn't collapse. It's like a goddamn cast-iron house of cards in there."

Norm said, "And with one of ours dead already, you're going to be expected to be especially cautious."

Nodding, Kraft sat on the edge of a desk. "The louvers are half off their damn hinges. We can't risk any explosives. Every chunk of rubble we remove has to come out by hand."

Latura looked at me. "And how long will their air hold?"

"Three hours," I said.

Kraft was nodding glumly. "Three hours, max."

"So," Latura said, "the people in the North Tunnel will only be four hours dead when you push through."

Deathly silence cloaked the room. Latura had made his point: the midway passage was no solution. It provided a means of evacuation for corpses only.

Latura said, "Somebody's got to go down there."

"And do what?" Kraft said skeptically.

"Cork it up. Block the fumes from the survivors till you *can* dig out the midriver. It would buy you the time you need."

"Cork it up?" Kraft asked. "Don't you mean, 'blow it up'?"

"You know what I mean, Frank. And you know it's the only reasonable course of action available to us. Hell, you're the acting chief, aren't you? Well, act."

Kraft swallowed. He wore the same constipated expression Norm had displayed earlier.

"Of course, if you do nothing," Latura said, "and play it

by the book, maybe you'd look better, if you have to testify later. *Maybe.*"

"That isn't fair, Kit," Kraft said.

You could feel the history between these two. It was like heat in the air, shimmering there.

"Clock is ticking, Frank," Latura said.

"Are you trying to run a guilt trip on me, Kit?"

"People are going to die, Frank. Again."

"That was the past. And that situation had nothing to do with me, and everything to do with *you.*"

"You're right. And I took the responsibility then, and I'm willing to take it now. I'll go to fucking prison if I have to, but one thing I won't do is stand in here yammering while those poor bastards are running out of air. Now, somebody has to *do* something, Frank."

Quietly, Kraft said, "You'd go in yourself?"

"I don't see any other hands in the air."

Kraft shook his head, turned to Norm. "You have a better suggestion? An alternate plan?"

Norm sighed. Shook his head no.

"Neither do I. But at least Latura *has* a plan." Kraft looked firmly at Norm. "Give him whatever he needs. Whatever he asks for."

And Latura and Kraft exchanged glances; Latura nodded, once—saying thanks, maybe. I'm not sure what it meant. But it meant something, something big, that glance.

"Question," Norm said. "If we don't have a way out of the North Tunnel, what makes you think we got a way *in?*"

Latura took centerstage. "When we ran the hypothetical in ninety-three, we formulated a last-resort plan of entry."

"I don't remember that," Norm said, "and I was there."

"We never actually ran that last-resort entry. We just discussed it. Worked it out."

"Why didn't you run it?"

Latura shrugged. "Somebody thought it was too dangerous. You know, to risk running in a hypothetical."

"Who?"

"Me."

A lot of wide-eyed glances got exchanged after *that* one.

Latura was pointing to the scale model, specifically to a
fan shaft. "There," he said.

Incredulous, Norm asked, "Go in through the exhaust
fans?"

Latura shrugged, took a deep breath. "Yeah." And he
gave the little model fan a spin with his index finger, making
it whir.

"The real ones are bigger, you know," I said.

"The first set of blades are mounted in the horizontal portion just beyond the mouth of the shaft," Norm was saying,
pointing to the scale model. "The other three sets of blades
are mounted in the vertical shaft below, beyond an elbow in
back of the first fan."

"Four sets of blades? Is that all?" Latura asked wryly.
Then he added, "Just as long as they're turned off when I
go in."

"Maybe the programming has changed since you ran your
hypothetical," I said, "but the way it is now, we can only
shut these fans down for three minutes."

Latura winced. "What?"

I nodded the sad truth. "We've got the intake fans all the
way up, to compensate, as best we can, for the exhaust drag.
When we shut that one down, it's going to severely cut the
oxygen in the North Tunnel. And when the oxygen gets too
low . . ."

"The computer automatically kicks the fans back on,"
Norm said. "Safety feature."

"Safety first," Latura said.

"There's another problem," I said.

"Oh, good. We wouldn't want this to be too easy."

"You won't come out on the roadway. You'll come out *under* it, in the intake duct."

Latura was frowning thoughtfully again. "Can you shut the fans down a second time?"

I shook my head no. "Not soon enough to do you any good, anyway. Norm, what's the combined force of those fans?"

"About a hundred sixty miles an hour," Norm said. "Give or take."

I said, "It'll be like a hurricane in there. You up for it?"

"It'll be like a vacation in Florida," Latura said. Gently sarcastic, he asked, "Do I have to punch my way through the roadway?"

"Close," I said. "There are manholes from the duct into the tunnel, every five hundred feet. You're going to have to get one open."

"I think I can shoulder a manhole cover open."

Norm said, "These lids weigh three hundred pounds."

"Give or take," Latura said.

"Get through one of them," I said, "and you're home free."

"When I'm in my BarcaLounger," Latura said, "with a cold one popped, *then* I'm home free." He turned to Frank Kraft and said, "Sounds like I'm gonna need Boom."

"I already sent for her," Kraft said.

"Then I guess it's time for you to introduce me to these big fans of mine," Latura said.

ASHLEY CRIGHTON

That nice black police officer, Mr. Tyrell, led us to where some other people were gathered, sitting on the elevated side-

78

walk in a place where the rail had got torn away.

There was this older couple named the Trillings—the woman was real happy, petting her dog that Officer Tyrell had found for her, but her husband seemed depressed, but like, who wasn't? (Their dog's name was Cooper—weird name for a dog, don't you think?) There was also a pretty woman who was probably about thirty whose clothes were grunged up from saving these four street kids who, we learned, were from a crashed bus that was taking them to reform school. That was all, except for Mom and Daddy and me.

Officer Tyrell was in charge, or at least he was till Roy Nord came strutting along.

I couldn't believe it! I recognized him from the commercials, right away! He was handsome, in a rugged Clint Eastwood sort of way but not as old, and he looked like he was ready to climb a mountain, ropes and gear and stuff draped all over him.

He seemed almost happy to be caught in a smoky tunnel. He had the same sort of perfect Crest toothpaste smile he had in his commercials.

Everybody recognized him, of course, except the Trillings, who said they only watched PBS. The tall black kid called Kadeem was really impressed, kept saying he had never seen a real live celebrity before. The girl named Latonya said Kadeem should stick around, maybe he'd see a real dead one.

Anyway, Roy Nord rounded us all up, Officer Tyrell, too, and said, "I may have found a way out, but I need help. Are you game?"

Kadeem raised a fist and grinned. "It's still out there!"

"What is?" Mrs. Trilling wondered. She didn't recognize that slogan from the Territory Beyond commercials, since they didn't play on PBS.

"Follow me," Roy Nord commanded.

Then he noticed me. At first I thought he was sizing me

77

up in that way guys do, you know? He had that same sort of horny look they get. Only he wasn't hot for me. He was hot for my video camera.

"Ashley," he said. "That's your name, isn't it?"

"Sure it's my name."

"Do you have tape in there, Beautiful?"

"Sure."

"Then when I tell you, start taping. It could be very valuable to both of us. People are curious about celebrities, and events like these."

"Disasters, you mean."

"Yes. They'll want to know just what we did to survive."

Dad said, "Are you *positive* you've found a way out?"

Roy Nord shook his head solemnly. "No. But it doesn't hurt to have hope. Hope never hurt anybody. Now, please, follow me, everyone."

And everybody did, like he was the Pied Piper, which I guess made us the rats, or maybe the mice.

We ended up at this spot where rubble was piled up from where a double doorway had caved in; the concrete and twisted metal and stuff came tumbling down over the elevated sidewalk. The rail was crushed under there somewhere.

But you could see in where it had caved in that there were some openings you could squeeze into and maybe through. If you were about the size of a poodle. Which even left that dog, Cooper, out.

But Roy Nord was gesturing to this pile of debris like he was showing off a new car (I was taping this, at his request, by the way).

"I've had a peek inside," he said, "and there are some nooks and crannies—let's call them wormholes—and they may add up to a way out of here. If you are praying people, pray. If you ever considered taking it up, now's a fine time to start."

Then he looked right at me.

I mean, my camera.

"And if there's a way out, I'll find it," he said, eyes all Clint Eastwood squinty. "Then we'll be where we belong—in the Territory Beyond."

A commercial! I was shooting a commercial! And here I thought I was entering the news field.

But the way the rest of our little group reacted, you'd think he was Abraham Lincoln giving the Gettysburg Address. Except for that pretty lady, Madelyne; she had a sort of skeptical expression.

Roy Nord went up to Kadeem; even though he was shorter, Roy Nord seemed taller. He put his hand on Kadeem's shoulder and said, "I'm going to need somebody to feed me the rope. You look like the man for the job."

Kadeem grinned. He bobbed around with some attitude. "Yeah, and haul your white ass out, if somethin' go wrong."

"Things don't go wrong for me," Roy Nord said. "There are no problems—Kadeem, is it? No problems in life. Just challenges . . . You up for this?"

"If I do," Kadeem said, "what's in it for me? Some of that shit in your commercials? I could use some shoes."

"Just make sure I get your sizes," Roy Nord said, smiling his movie-star smile. Then he turned and looked at each of us. "Goes for all of you."

"All right!" Vincent said, and there was some general laughter.

Roy Nord was so confident, it made everybody feel better. It was like the tension eased up.

Officer Tyrell stepped forward. "If Nord here has some luck," he said, "I want to make sure we've got all the survivors rounded up. . . . I'm going to make one last sweep."

Then he handed his walkie-talkie to Madelyne.

"I've been trying to raise communication and getting

nothing but static," he said, "but keep trying for me, would you? I'll be back."

Madelyne nodded, taking the walkie-talkie, and Officer Tyrell went jogging off down the tunnel. She kept trying to get somebody on it while Roy Nord and Kadeem got started getting the ropes and stuff hooked up at the mouth of that caved-in double doorway.

CATHY "BOOM" DIX, EMS

I linked up with Chief Latura in the ventilation building, a many-louvered cement-floored chamber, as cold as the outside, dominated by the huge duct bearing a gigantic fan behind grillwork that looked like Paul Bunyan's window fan. And it wasn't noisy in there, oh no, not any more than an airfield with the Blue Angels warming up.

This plan sounded crazy enough for the chief, and if anybody could pull it off, he could. I dug out a little something special for him, out of my locker, where I'd kept it stowed all this time.

He was standing with Frank Kraft and a handsome thir-tyish black woman I later learned was named Grace Lincoln, from the communications center in the New Jersey Tunnel Building. They were standing to one side of the huge churning fan, and somebody hit a switch and the grillwork over the shaft retracted, making room for some fool to crawl inside.

Seeing me, the fool in question half smiled and ambled over.

"Hi, Cathy," he said.

He was always the only one on the job who called me that.

"I loaded this old piece of shit up for you," I told him,

handing him the explosives-packed vest, which just happened to be his old duty vest with CHIEF LATURA stenciled on the back.

"You're a sentimental soul, Cathy," he said, taking the vest, slipping it on. "I would've thought they'd've shredded this SOB by now."

"I saved it. Regular pack rat. Can't bring myself to throw any old piece of garbage out. That sucker's loaded. No smokin', now."

He grinned at me. "What am I packing on this fine evening?"

"Semtex. You need a refresher on the procedure?"

"Set, wire, contact . . . run like a son of a bitch?"

"What a memory on the guy."

He shook his head, still grinning.

"Here," I said, and handed him a throat-mounted walkietalkie. "You're gonna wanna keep in touch, cowboy."

"Thanks."

He began running through the channels—you know, EMS, NYPD, fire department, tunnel and bridge agent command post, tunnel cops . . . and suddenly he raised somebody.

". . . can anybody hear me?" the walkie-talkie squawked, a woman's voice.

"I hear you," the chief said. To me he said, "Shit, this is somebody in the tunnel." Then into his throat mount he said, "Who's *this*?"

"Jesus Christ!" the woman's voice said.

I said, "You meet the most interesting people in this line of work."

"You can *hear* me?" the woman's voice continued. Then she seemed to call somebody: "George! *George!*"

Later we learned that George Tyrell was the officer down there.

Chief Latura said, "Talk to me! How many people are alive down there?"

"Eleven, no twelve . . . and a dog. We're all at the middle of the tunnel. There's a man down here who thinks he's found a way out."

The chief frowned at me as he snapped, "How? Where?"

"Some kind of big doorway that's caved in . . ."

Her voice was breaking up.

"Midriver passage," Chief Latura muttered. His face was very tight. "Now listen to me carefully. Tell this man not to go in there. Under no circumstances go in there. All of you need to sit tight—help is on the way. Can you do that?"

But the only reply from the walkie-talkie was static.

"Shit," the chief said.

I followed him over to Deputy Chief Kraft and this Lincoln woman, who had a cell phone in hand.

"Ready when you are, boys and girls," the chief said to them.

Lincoln said, "Once I give the word, you got three minutes. These fans are timed logarithmically. Fan One kicks on after one minute. The remaining three in forty-second intervals. Follow?"

"You're saying I don't have much time."

"Roger that. Look . . . there's a tunnel cop down there named George Tyrell—you tell him I want my damn bracelet back, okay?"

The chief nodded, reached out, and squeezed her hand. She lifted the phone to her face.

"Ready to shut down," she said into the cell phone, "on my prompt."

Chief Latura was snugging on climbing gloves as Deputy Chief Kraft approached him. I suppose it was meant to be a private moment, but Kraft had to speak up to be heard over that churning fan, and that meant I heard him, too.

"Kit," he said, "what I did, I did for the good of the department. It wasn't personal."

"Frank," Chief Latura said, "he was your brother. It doesn't get more personal than that."

"I was angry. I'm . . . Kit, I'm sorry. You always were a good man."

"Christ, Frank, this is starting to sound like a eulogy. Don't you think I'm coming back?" Then he looked into the huge whirling blades of the fan. "Don't answer that."

He poised himself to crawl into the fan duct. On his belt was a coil of climbing rope, though he wouldn't be using it; the fans below were the rocks of the mountain he was climbing down.

"Talking about shit hitting the fan," the chief said, then added: "Let's do it."

And Grace Lincoln said one word into her cell phone: *"Now!"*

6

FAN DANCE

In the control room, Norman Bassett sat at his computer and threw the switches that would begin a wild ride for former EMS Chief Kenneth "Kit" Latura, who could hear Bassett's voice on the walkie-talkie in a side/rear pocket of his explosives-laden vest as he waited to walk into the blades of the sixteen-foot-in-diameter fan.

"Fan Two . . . down.

"Fan Three . . . down.

"Fan Four . . . down!"

And as the fan before him ground to a halt, Latura ducked into the duct and faced the still-slowing blades; a computerized beeping could be heard both in the control room and in the ventilation shaft Latura was entering, an electronic pulse that provided the bold volunteer with an aural reminder of the clock he was trying to beat.

Latura gripped a blade, stopped the slowing fan, began

working his way methodically but quickly through the first set of them, huge old blades, greasy, cobwebbed curves of pitted metal. Soon he was past them and at the edge of the elbow where the duct made its sudden sharp downward turn; he peered over the metal precipice and could see, below, the first set of blades in the vertical shaft.

Behind him, that first fan kicked back on with a vicious velocity that would have swept him back into those churning blades had he not first hurled himself off the elbow, landing five feet below, on his back, on one large stopped blade of the second set of fan blades, like an insect landing on a leaf of steel.

But the aerodynamics of the moving fan above had its effect on this set of fans, and turned off or not, Latura's bed of steel began rotating. It was as if he were riding a giant turntable, wind whipping through the shaft, the electronic beeping pulse continuing, the red LED readouts of the computerized air sensors (mounted by each set of blades) ticking off tenths of seconds, grains of sand streaming through the neck of an oh-so-very-tiny hourglass, and it was under these conditions that Latura had to find his balance, and press on.

Slipping through the greasy pitted blades, he lowered himself through them and in a stiff-armed position, as if he were on the parallel bars, he suspended himself within the shaft, like some piece of human refuse caught there.

It was at this point that he heard the voice of Madelyne Thompson coming from his pocketed walkie-talkie; there was no doubt static and breakup, but Thompson confirmed their conversation, and it must have taken place at this point.

"Excuse me," she said. "Am I catching you at a bad time?"

Into his throat mike, Latura said, "Talk to me."

"I just thought you should know that I passed along what

you said, about not going in there, but that guy went in, anyway. In the midriver passage?''

''Who? Who's gone in?''

That was the extent of the conversation, and perhaps it was best that it got cut off there, because at this juncture, Latura had seven seconds left.

He dropped down, hanging from the O-ring supporting the fan's impellers. The third set of fan blades was a mere three feet below, but on those curved blades, a tricky drop nonetheless; easy to crack an ankle, or get gashed by a blade— dull or not, those blades could cut you, if you fell hard on them and/or at the wrong angle.

The motor for the second set of blades, where he was presently perched, kicked back on, and Latura let go.

He landed with the grace of an acrobat, balancing himself by stepping gingerly on two blades. But any sense of security soon went out from under him as again he found himself on a moving turntable. The blades he straddled were suddenly turning, not via electricity, but from the seventy-mile wind the screaming fans above were generating, a wind that was whipping him savagely.

And the LED read: 32 . . . 31 . . . 30 . . .

He lowered himself carefully through the gently moving blades of the third set of fans; four below was the final set. As he made his way the speed of the fan blades through which he was wending began to accelerate as the fans above shrieked and wind blasted through the funnel.

And the LED read: 18 . . . 17 . . . 16 . . .

He was almost through when his explosives vest snagged somewhere behind him, on a blade. He tried to maneuver free, but he was hooked on a buckled piece of strap iron right where his walkie-talkie was pocketed. The bulk of his detonators were ringed back there, too.

And the LED read: 9 . . . 8 . . . 7 . . .

Latura withdrew a hunting knife from his belt and reached behind him and sliced off his back pocket in one, clean stroke.

The walkie-talkie and all but one of his thumb detonators clattered through the fans below, down through the shaft, gone forever.

The motor for the third set of fans kicked in, and Latura dropped down gracelessly to the final set of fans. Just four feet above, the Cuisinart of fans whirled over his head.

Estimates put the airflow, at this point, at around one hundred miles per hour, which drove the inert fan he was now straddling as if it were a 78-record turntable. At this speed, Latura's nausea must have been incredible.

Dizzy, sick, Latura managed to take his climbing rope from his belt, keeping it in his left hand as he worked his way between the churning blades, upside down, until his upper torso was through the last set of fans. His weight slowed the turntable, but it was still moving as he tried to focus on a place where he could fasten the hook end of his rope.

He tried to secure it to the steel axle in the middle of the fan, but the inner O-ring kept it agonizingly out of reach. He tried again, and again, the wind vicious now, even his weight not slowing the turntable much, and he could not just let go, because a ten-story drop into the blackness of a conical funnel was all that was waiting for him below.

And the LED read: 4 . . . 3 . . . 2 . . .

The rumble of the final motor kicking in told Latura he had no choice; he whipped his rope through the figure eight on his harness, slammed the hook on the O-ring, and dove headfirst into darkness.

Grabbing hold of the rope in his right, gloved hand, Latura dropped through the shaft like a spider scrambling for safety. How Latura managed it with one arm, however powerful that arm may have been, is one for the record books, somewhere on the same page where a mother lifts a Buick off her baby; but he did it, he used the strength of one arm to break his fall, and finally, as he neared the end of his rope, literally, he snapped into an upright position, his glove smoking from the friction of the fall.

At that instant the centrifugal force of the rope carried by the spinning blade threw him back out to the wall of the shaft, as if he were holding on to the tail of a cracking whip, slamming him, banging him brutally into the rounded ductwork.

What follows is difficult to grasp but apparently true. Latura somehow managed to kick off against the sides of the shaft and began to use the centrifugal force to his advantage, and began running the circumference of the shaft, virtually running horizontally to keep from dropping, corkscrewing down, down, down the conical funnel.

But finally he was falling, dropping, and he clanged like a clapper in a bell against a steel wall, and began tumbling, getting sucked headfirst right into a hole straight below.

Latura emerged from that hole into the bottom half of the funnel, under the roadbed, as Grace Lincoln had briefed him. At the far end was a six-hole manifold; between him and that, in a violent cyclone of fan-whipped air, flew the detritus of seventy years—gum wrappers, newspaper fragments, bottle caps—a snowstorm of schmutz shot around in a gale-force wind.

He flew into this gusty hell and, like just another large chunk of refuse, got hurled around, smacking flat against the center two holes of the manifold, the suction of which was enormous, like the back end of a giant vacuum cleaner. Had he been sucked through those holes, Latura's rescue mission would have been over.

And so would Latura.

But as we already know, Latura's physical strength was quite remarkable, and he summoned it to do a spread-eagled push-up that got him away from those holes, and in one nimble move he flipped over and dropped down to the curvature of the tube below.

The winds down there were as chaotic as above, lifting him up, legs first. He slammed his hands down on the lowest rung of two ladders that were inset on each side of the tube, providing working access for a manhole and for a junction box.

Hand over hand, Latura pulled himself up the ladder, unable to get a footing, legs pulled straight out as he climbed using only his upper torso, waving there like a human flag. Finally he managed to swing his legs around and lock them inside the top rung of the ladder.

He was under the manhole cover now. Even with his considerable strength, he didn't bother trying to budge the three-hundred-pound lid. He took from his vest an aluminum box containing a block of Semtex and peeled back the foil on the end to expose the plastic explosive, discarding the foil to free it to fly with the other imprisoned wind-whipped rubbish.

Then Latura withdrew his only remaining thumb detonator from the ragged vest, planting the wire in the brick of plastic explosive, removing the paper from the sticky fastening surface, and—doing a sit-up in the cyclone—stretched out to plant the canister of Semtex under the manhole cover.

Latura unspooled his wire as he moved back down the ladder, the howling wind whipping the wire around like a ship's rigging in a storm. He held the detonator, safety on, between his teeth.

Safely positioned at the bottom of the tube, he snapped the safety off and the detonator went hot.

I don't watch TV that much, I be a workin' girl, but sometime I sit with Nordell and watch, mostly Big Bird and Bert and Ernie and shit. But sure, I seen this Roy Nord before, climbin' and hikin' and sellin' shoes and T-shirts and that.

Famous people don't impress me much, I trick some baseball and football stars in my time, but I did like seein' Roy Nord go in that hole and look for a way out. Kind of give us all a lift, some hope, you know?

Only it start to go sour, real fast.

This white guy name Steven something, with the wife and the girl about my age who got a camera and is always recordin' us and shit? He go over where Kadeem is feedin' rope in that hole where it be all cave in, where that Roy Nord go crawlin' inside.

This Steven, he edge by Kadeem and holler in, "Nord! You see anything?"

And Kadeem kind of push the white guy back, like somebody die and make him king. "Shut up. You wanna cause a cave-in, chump?"

"I have a right to know what's going on," Steven say. But his voice, it was kind of shakin'.

"Get back from here," Kadeem say. "Let the man concentrate."

That good-lookin' greaser, Vincent, he was kind of hangin' with Kadeem. When he lean in and look in the hole, Kadeem don't say anything. At first.

But then Vincent, he make a mistake. He raise some doubt and doubt ain't what Kadeem wants to hear right now, 'cause you know what? I think Kadeem, he as scared as any of us.

Anyway, Vincent lean in the hole, lookin' in there.

"Maybe he's not comin' back," Vincent say.

"He be back, all right," Kadeem say.

"If you got through, would *you* come back? He's been gone a long time. I wanna try myself."

"No. Get back away from there."

"You sayin' you gone to stop me if I wanna go in myself?"

Kadeem's eyes, they be narrow and cold in his face. "That's right. Go ahead, spic. Move on me. I love for you to do that. . . ."

Vincent back off, but all of a sudden everybody's talkin' about maybe they should try it. Madelyne says no, that some rescue worker say we shoulden go in there. But nobody pay her no nevermind.

The older white guy, Roger, the one with the wife and the dog, he come forward and say, "Women and children first. That's the way it's done."

Kadeem kinda start to swagger and shit. "Oh, you done this before? How many tunnels you been trap in?"

Vincent say, "Hey, I'm a juvie. I vote yes on this children-first shit."

And Vincent start to move toward that opening, only Kadeem pull him away, give him a badass shove. Vincent bump into Steven, and people start yellin' at each other. We about two seconds away from people swingin' at each other when somethin' bigger than somebody's temper blew up.

Sound like the world explode.

ROY NORD
(excerpt from cell-phone transcript)

Serena? Do we have enough signal to record? Good. This will be short.

I'm in a clearing about the size of a walk-in closet. So far I've been able to crawl smoothly but slowly through the wreckage. The cave-in left numerous crawl spaces, but it's tight, dark, and claustrophobic in here. I feel like a flea trying to navigate a closed fist. Don't try this at home.

This closetlike opening is the most room I've come onto so far. Above me are huge steel louvers that *were* anchored by chains from alternating sides of a ventilation shaft. I'd say it was an aerodynamic manifold. Now, however, they're blown completely out of position, the top louver some two hundred feet above me resting precariously on the one below, and others are hanging equally askew off of their respective pivots.

Swords of Damocles.

The other side of this passage, in the direction that would have led us to the South Tunnel had fate been more kind, is totally blocked, primarily by a slab of concrete that Superman couldn't lift. The only way out is above—the ventilation shaft.

Not exactly inviting—but I've seen worse.

MADELYNE THOMPSON

Things were getting ugly. Roy Nord had been gone only for ten minutes, but it seemed much longer, and those street kids started shoving each other around, and even the Trillings and the Crightons seemed to be considering exploring that wormhole themselves.

I tried to convey what the rescue worker on the walkie-talkie had indicated about the danger of the midriver passage, but no one paid any attention. Can you blame them? What other option did they have? The air was thinning and polluted by smoke. Desperation was clawing at us, like a small feral animal.

If Officer Tyrell would just get back, I figured some order could be restored, and then maintained. Edging out into the tunnel, I looked for him. Finally Officer Tyrell, his flashlight doing a Luke Skywalker through the smoky haze, came moving up the tunnel toward me, and I felt a surge of hope. The sight of him was a reassuring one, even if he was moving past cars with charred corpses in them.

Suddenly, not far behind Officer Tyrell, a huge explosion cannoned one of those cars over on its side, and a manhole cover went flying like a wicked discus, clattering against the tiled wall, carving a gouge out like a scar, and from where the car used to be, and where the manhole cover beneath that car had been, came a figure, rising up in a column of smoke like Orpheus returning from the land of the dead.

That stopped the bickering faster than even Officer Tyrell might have.

Tyrell had hit the deck, and now was getting to his feet as I walked briskly down to him where our new addition had paused to look back at the toxic fire, uptunnel—it seemed to flare up for his benefit. Then our visitor loped up to us; he wore a khaki vest over a white shirt and dark slacks, and his smudged face was darkly, roughly handsome, in a slightly battered sort of way. His eyes were hooded, and had a mournful cast, yet they were sharp, and not without humor.

"Are you part of the rescue team?" I asked him, handing Tyrell his walkie-talkie back.

"I *am* the rescue team." He shook hands with Tyrell and then with me. "Kit Latura, Emergency Search and Rescue out of Emergency Medical Services."

"I've heard of you," Tyrell said. He was studying our one-man rescue team with an oddly glazed expression; he seemed wary and respectful all at once. "How long have you been back with EMS?"

"About an hour." To me, he said, "Are you the woman I spoke to?"

"Yes."

His face clenched in a flick of a frown. "I thought I made it clear that nobody was to go in that passage."

"I passed the word along," I said defensively. "Nobody listened to me. It's a little tense in here, in case you haven't noticed."

"Sorry."

We had made it to the midriver passage, now, and our little group gathered about us.

"Where's the rest of the rescue crew?" Vincent asked.

"You're looking at it," Latura said.

"Shit!" Latonya said. "Man, that can't be right. You're it? You are it?"

"Budget cuts," Latura said wryly.

Roger Trilling, holding his wife's hand as she petted her pooch's head, said, "Can you lead us out the way you came in?"

Latura shook his head no. "I came down a treacherous fan shaft with blades that could only be shut off for a matter of seconds at a time. I'm highly trained at this sort of thing, and barely made it through alive myself. I'm sorry, but we have to find another way."

"Somebody beat you to it," Steven Crighton said, pointing to the caved-in passage.

"I don't think so," Latura said. He nodded up the rubble pile, toward where Kadeem manned the rope. "How many are in there?"

I said, "There's only—"

"Hey!" Kadeem snapped. "He's talkin' to me, woman.

You mind?" Then to Latura, Kadeem said, "There's only one man in there—Roy Nord hisself—"

Latura frowned. "The guy in the commercials?"

"Yeah," Tyrell said, moving in next to Latura. "He had the back of his HumVee loaded down with climbing gear. He came prepared."

"There's no preparation for something like this," Latura said. To Kadeem he said, "Excuse me."

Then Latura climbed up the rubble and shouted in the wormhole: "Emergency Search and Rescue! Please climb back out, *now!*"

Steven Crighton stepped forward, positioning himself at the foot of the rubble pile, and said, "Hold it right there. Do *you* have a way out for us?"

Latura ignored the question, calling into the wormhole. "This shaft is extremely unstable. Please climb back out immediately!"

The only response was silence.

Kadeem put his hand on Latura's shoulder and Latura's look back at him was as coldly menacing as Kadeem's was hot and bothered.

"Yo, man—what's up with you? *I'm* the man got left in charge here."

Crighton began up the rubble pile. "He's right. Roy Nord's finding us safe passage...."

Latura flicked Kadeem's hand off like a bothersome insect, and he turned and the force of his personality was like a blast from a furnace.

"Everybody back the hell off! Back off and listen carefully—that whole shaft in there has been damaged. Try going through and it'll come down on top of you like a collapsing building."

"Well," Crighton said, "since you've just joined our little

party, let me bring you up to speed—it's not exactly fucking safe in here, either!''

Little Mikey, sitting on the elevated sidewalk, whined, "We can't hardly breathe, man!"

"I know that," Latura said calmly, gently. "I know you've already been put through hell down here, but I have to ask for your patience, and your courage. Hang in there just a little longer, and trust me."

Latura began to move down the rubble pile, and Kadeem got in his way.

"Roy on top of this," Kadeem said.

"Unless he's very lucky," Latura said, "Roy is going to be under it. Now stand aside, please—I don't want to have to go through you."

Kadeem sneered, snorted, threw a punch that Latura deftly ducked, then in a move so quick I can't really describe it, Latura slipped an arm around Kadeem's neck, twisting, taking control of various pressure points.

"Choose," Latura said coolly, keeping the lanky kid in the choke hold. "You can, A, go to sleep and miss all the fun, or you can, B, stay up late and be helpful."

It took a while for Kadeem to cave, and his eyes looked like they were going to roll back as he came close to passing out; but the kid finally said, "B . . . B!"

"Good choice," Latura said, and released him. Without missing a beat, Latura stripped off his vest and handed it to Officer Tyrell.

"Explosives," he told the officer. "TLC treatment, okay?"

"You got it," Tyrell said.

Then Latura scrambled back up the rubble and was inside the wormhole, following Roy Nord's rope.

7

TERRITORY BEYOND

Just at the moment Latura was entering the wormhole of the midriver passage, the tunnel—not far from where the survivors stood squabbling over whether the voice of reason belonged to Roy Nord or Kit Latura—was suffering a sort of cerebral hemorrhage.

Over the roadway, along where the roof met the curve of the tunnel, wall tiles began to undulate almost sensuously, like a cobra rising from a basket at the beckoning of a seductive native flute.

Then came a pop, another pop, and another, as tiles came flying off, and the walls were suddenly bleeding brown water as the river began seeping its way into the tunnel.

Latura was unaware that the tunnel had begun springing major leaks as he pulled himself into the wormhole, a wire-wrapped bulkhead light burning at the end of a mangled electrical conduit providing unexpected illumination.

The small succor of this was overshadowed by two things:
a hiss, and a smell, which told Latura of another leakage—
gas.

Inching forward, he was able to see a Con Ed gas main
with a split seam; the cracked pipe ran parallel to the wall
on the other side of which was the elevated sidewalk. If it
blew, it might take the survivors on the other side of that
wall with it.

As if he needed hastening, Latura hustled along the rope
trail that indicated Roy Nord's passage.

ROY NORD
(excerpt from cell-phone transcript)

Serena? Recording? Can you hear over this damn hissing
sound? Fine . . .

I'm positioned on the first louver in the shaft. It was a
fifty-foot climb up a cliff of rubble to get to the point where
I could leap over an eight-foot drop to this steel plate. Now
it's just a matter of scaling up to the next one.

Okay, Serena, this next is FYI only.

In, oh, about half an hour, I'll be leading these survivors
up through this ventilation shaft, including some inner-city
teenagers, which is nice, since that's a major market we
haven't penetrated as well as I feel we should. And these
gang kids love expensive running shoes, so there's no reason
. . . anyway, this could build our image among nonwhite con-
sumers.

I should still be able to make the Teterboro flight, so be
a doll, and alert the press they can talk to me at the Denver
layover.

Bye for now.

They was all arguin' about who was right, Roy Nord or the rescue guy, Latura, and while they was busy gettin' in each other's face, I walk up that rubble pile and Kadeem says, "What the fuck you think you're doin'?"

"I'm goin' in," I says, and that's what I do, slip right in that hole and figure if Kadeem wants to let go of that rope and come in after me, let him try. See who's got the bigger balls, him or me.

There's some kind of hangin' light in there, it's dim, but you can see, and I trace along the rope, and right away I'm behind him, Latura, in the bottom of this shaft. Rubble all around, but there's nooks and there's crannies you could think about squeezin' through, and you can see up this shaft, and there's these big metal slats on both sides, connected by these chains, like some humongous window blinds, and way up there, maybe fifty, sixty feet, Roy Nord's perched, with all his mountain-climber shit?

And Latura, he's leanin' against some rubble, lookin' up at Roy Nord, and he's talkin' real calm, real nice and easy, like he's tryin' to talk some suicidal nut to come in off a buildin' ledge.

"Mr. Nord," he says, and I don't even know if he notice I'm behind him yet, "my name is Latura. EMS. I'm askin' you to get down off of there, right now."

And Roy Nord calls down, and it sounds just like his voice on TV, 'cause it's like in an echo chamber, sounds all cool and shit, and anyway Nord says, "That sounds like you're issuing an order, Mr. Latura. If you'd like to place an order, I'll give you my eight-hundred number."

That made me laugh, and Latura turned and looked at me

and says, "Get the hell out of here, while you can!"

And I say, "Bullshit—I'm ready, now!"

Roy Nord's up there, riggin' his climbin' harness, gettin' ready to go up them big old steel slats, like a big metal ladder only some of the rungs are fucked up. He looked down at me and Latura and says, "Lead, follow, or get out of my way."

"There's no way out through this shaft," Latura calls up.

And the whole structure, it was creakin' and groanin' like a really old man takin' a dump. I admit I was havin' second thoughts about this whole deal.

But I stand my ground. How would it look, if I come runnin' scaredy-ass out of there?

Latura was still tryin'. "Mr. Nord—this entire shaft is a house of cards. If it comes down, they'll spend months sifting through rubble looking for the pieces of you."

"If you worked for me," Roy Nord calls down, in a dissin' kind of way, "I'd fire you for that attitude."

"It's not an attitude. It's facts. You can't will this away, you can't wish this away!"

Roy Nord was gettin' his line all set so he could scale up to the next slat. But before he did, he gives this little speech.

He says, "This shaft is not going to collapse. How do I know? Because Roy Nord has a sixth sense. You don't achieve what I've achieved in life without developing an instinct for the dynamics of a given situation. Do you actually imagine I'm going to ignore my instincts in favor of the gutless whining of some . . . some *paramedic*? Get real!"

"You'll never make it."

"I *always* make it. . . ."

But there was an awful wrenchin' sound from above, like maybe the shaft don't agree with him.

"As soon as I get these ropes in place," Roy Nord says,

"you start bringing the others in—and tell that sweet young thing not to forget her damn camera!"

I could barely see him up there now, so much dust got stirred up. It was hazy, like bad fog.

"Get out of here," Latura says to me.

"No," I say, "he's makin' it!"

And he was! The dust fog cleared enough so's I could see him. He had his ropes rigged up double, like a mountain climber, and what's the word for it? What? Rappel? If you say so.

He go rappellin' up to the next slat and then, Jesus, it was *awful....*

The chain holdin' the first slat to the one above him, it snapped, just like that, like a finger snap, and this awesome chain reaction started, those big steel slats crashin' down, and above him, twenty, thirty tons more of those steel slats come spillin' right down on him.

All of this I see in just a flash, but my mind must of took a mental picture, 'cause sometimes I still wake up sweatin', seein' those giant steel knives come tumblin' down at me....

I get another flash of Roy Nord, jumpin' off that slat, shimmyin' down toward us, then lettin' go and droppin' down the last eight feet or so, to the floor of the pit.

Meantime, Latura pushed me! Pushed me hard, pushed me out of the way and he was right after me, makin' me move faster than I knew I could move.

The sound, Christ! I never heard nothin' like it, like the loudest heavy-metal band you ever heard fallin' off a cliff and playin' all the way down, grindin' steel and crushin' concrete and shit, oh man!

And Roy Nord, he was at the bottom of it. Underneath it all. All those steel slats, they came down on him like in that game in the arcade, you ever play that? Tetris? Where the slabs and blocks and chunks of shit come droppin' down and you got to stack them or die? Well, these son of a bitches stacked themselves right on him, and he was the bottom slab.

He was probably dead, though, when that first one hit him.

And those nooks and crannies I told you about? They started goin' away, fillin', disappearin'; once that steel fell, the rock and other shit come crashin' down and makin' somethin' else crash down and, man, it was like deadly dominoes.

This Latura, he grabbed onto me, pulled me after him, and he ran, and moved, duckin' and dodgin', like he was carryin' the ball through heavy-duty defense. We was just roundin' this sort of triangle-shape hole between slabs when where we was movin' down got a ton of rubble dumped on it.

So he turns, still yankin' me, and we got a sort of straight-away in front of us now. A narrow path we can cut down. He's out front, and we can still see, sort of, even though there's damn dust everywhere, 'cause of some hangin' light that somehow or other made it through all this shit, but it's a ways away and where we're runnin' is awful dim and all this fallin' rock and steel is makin' a terrible noise, it's roarin' like a hungry beast and I ain't never been so scared.

I'm lookin' back at the world cavin' in behind us and Latura yells, "Go! Go! Go!" and pulls me along and shoves me through another opening and we're back around where we started, we can hear that hissin' sound, and that light is brighter, and there's the light of the tunnel, the place I came in through, but everything's shakin', like a earthquake, dust cloudin' up, bits and pieces and even chunks of concrete rainin' on us faster and faster and faster. . . .

I can't hardly see, the dust and debris is a shitstorm, but Latura, he put his shoulder into me and we go flyin' out the opening, tumblin' down the hill of rubble past where Kadeem was standin', and funny thing, even with dust in my eyes and movin' that fast, I seen somethin' nobody but me would of picked up on. . . . Kadeem was standin' to one side of that hole, like he was waitin' to help us, but he had a pipe in his hand, held close to his chest where nobody could see the way he was standin'? And five'll get you ten he planned to bash Latura on the skull with it.

But that never happened.

Instead, this big mother of a gas explosion blew out of where we tumbled out of like a damn dragon belched, you never saw such a blossom of fire and debris going every which way, man!

And it caught everybody off guard, but nobody more off guard than Kadeem.

The damn blast blew him back clean across the roadway, across the tunnel, and smashed his ass into the tile wall. Then it sat him down, *whump!*

And then it was like he was just sittin' there, nice and quiet, takin' a break. Only there was eight inches of steel bar stickin' out of his chest, like when the alien jumped out of that guy in the movie.

And Kadeem looked down at it, his orange prison threads turnin' a nasty red, and he had this disappointed look, like some kid that got his favorite toy busted.

MADELYNE THOMPSON

Kit Latura had more presence of mind than anyone I've ever met. He comes scrambling out of that cave-in, then when an explosion bursts out after him, a *second* after him at most, he has control enough to shout, "Get down!" even as he leaps on top of me.

So we're in, basically, this missionary position as the explosion continues, and under him, shielding my own eyes, I saw the gas-main blast as it made its terrible way down the wall, tiles erupting from above the elevated sidewalk as the compressive explosion tore along the wall, as when somebody pulls wiring through a plaster wall, in a straight line, tracing an inexorable path toward New Jersey, where, out of sight from us but never out of mind, its toxic big brother continued to rage.

But before long it was over. Some fire, plenty of smoke, remained; but the explosion had spent itself.

Dust drifted almost lazily down as we began reassembling ourselves. The Trillings' dog, Cooper, had run off somewhere, and was now adding his plaintive howl to an already somber atmosphere.

Latura was on top of me, looking down at me; I was suddenly aware of my breasts being crushed against his chest, and I wouldn't file sexual harassment against the guy or anything, but it was definitely time for him to get off me.

"Are you okay?" he said.

I gave him a nudge, and he got the point, and rolled off as I said, "Do I look okay?"

He shrugged. "You look fine."

"I look fine?" I gestured to the smudged, disheveled person I'd become. "I'll have you know, I feel far from fine. Nowhere near fine, or for that matter, anywhere near the fucking outskirts of okay."

"You're welcome," he said.

On his feet now, he offered me a hand, which I was not too proud to take.

He looked me over. "You got two arms, two legs, your mouth still works," Latura said. "I'd say you're okay. Fine, even."

We both had a look around, appraising the aftermath of the explosion. For one thing, that wormhole was definitely not going to provide us with a way out. Mostly, no one looked much the worse for wear. Vincent was still on the cement, on his stomach, heaving for breath, obviously scared shitless. The Crightons were huddled together, Mom and Dad checking over their daughter's well-being (''Moth-er! I'm *fine*!''). Eleanor Trilling was downtunnel a ways, trying to coax Cooper off from his perch on top of a charred car. Mikey was helping her.

''Okay, Cooper,'' she was saying. ''It's okay, baby. I'm right here. Come down to mother—please?''

The dog wasn't cooperating, despite her outstretched arms; he just kept up his mournful howl.

She called out to her husband, ''Roger! Cooper is terrified out of his *wits*! Come here and *talk* to him! Roger?''

Her husband's reply echoed down the tunnel: ''In a damn *minute,* Eleanor!''

Roger and Latonya were kneeling over by where Kadeem seemed to be sitting by the wall across from where the mid-river passage opening used to be.

Only he wasn't ''just'' sitting. . . .

''Damn,'' Latura said, and he moved over there quickly.

So did I.

The boy had a good eight inches of rebar protruding from his chest. And his orange prison jumpsuit was stained scarlet.

Latura bent over the lanky kid, who seemed more in shock than in pain.

Kadeem's mouth was foaming blood as he uttered, ''Can't some . . . body shut up that damn dog?''

''Shhh,'' Latura told him. ''Don't talk.''

''You . . . you a medic, ain't ya, man? Can ya . . . do anything?''

Latonya, her cold face streaked with tears, said, ''He said be quiet, fool. You wanna get better? Stay still.''

Kadeem spoke to Latura: ''You can't help me, man?''

Latura sighed, shook his head no. ''I won't lie to you.'' He put a hand on Kadeem's shoulder.

"I can't . . . I can't *die,* man. I ain't hardly lived."

Covering her face, Latonya walked away, sobbing.

Roger Trilling said, "Is there anyone you want us to call? To contact?"

"Tell . . . tell my father, man. Tell him I was like, you know—tryin' to help people down here . . . help 'em get home and shit."

"Well that's true," Latura said. "You were."

"We'll tell your father his son was a hero," Trilling said.

Something brightened in his eyes. "You tell him that?"

"Yes, we will," Trilling said.

Latura nodded, patted the kid's shoulder.

"We'll find him," Trilling continued, "and we'll tell him."

Kadeem laughed once, bubbling blood. "He won't believe you, man. . . ."

Then the eyes weren't bright anymore.

Latura reached out and closed Kadeem's eyelids.

Then that boy Vincent that Latura had pulled out of the wormhole with him was standing there, looking down at Kadeem with glazed eyes and a humorless little smile.

"Guess ol' Roy Nord did lead Kadeem outta the tunnel, after all," the boy said.

GRACE LINCOLN

Within minutes of losing communication with Latura, our control room at the New Jersey River Building had been converted into Command Central, yellowed architectural plans of the tunnel taped wherever the walls allowed. Our little interconnecting cubbyholes were a beehive of activity, with city engineers, construction and demolition experts, and various political liaisons crowding around, moving through, considering options and flat out arguing, which is what happens when the options you have to explore are so lousy. Deputy Chief Kraft was present; so was Latura's friend, the woman they called Boom.

Norm Bassett was the first to know. From my monitors, I couldn't see it, or tell, so when he came running in, that was when I heard.

"Shut up, everybody!" Norm yelled. "Shut the hell up! . . . The midriver passage just collapsed, and a gas main has blown—and which is cause, and which is effect, at this point is only guesswork."

The room, bustling before, was deathly silent now.

Norm said, "Anyway, that passage is now completely blocked—the whole infrastructure has come crashing down. We don't know yet whether anyone was in there at the time. . . ."

"Anything from the chief yet?" Boom asked.

"No. Nothing since we lost contact in the fan shaft."

I thought he'd fallen, I really did; I figured he was already dead. And Boom, tough little gal, her eyes were all watery, lower lip trembling; she must have had the same gut-wrenching suspicion.

"It may be as simple as he dropped his walkie-talkie on the way down," Norm said.

"Never write off the chief," Boom said tightly, quaveringly. "*Never* write him off."

"We got a leak in that tunnel," I said, pointing to one of the few still-functioning monitors.

Deathly silence again.

"Look at the bright side," Boom said. "Maybe the water will put out the fire."

A few grim chuckles followed that gallows humor, but I couldn't make myself join in.

"God help them," I said, shaking my head, holding the tears back somehow. "Now there's no way out."

8

TABLOID NEWS

Whether Roy Nord's efforts were noble and bold, as some have written, or self-serving and arrogant, as other commentators have maintained, two things are inarguable: those efforts killed him; and the avalanche of steel, cement, and detritus he caused within the ventilation shaft led to ruinous aftershocks, beginning with the gas-main explosion.

The last aftershock of Roy Nord's hubris was perhaps the worst: uptunnel from the survivors, swollen tiles burst from the walls in an Uzi-like barrage, and tendrils of murky brown riverwater clawing down those ravaged walls quickly turned into something fiercer, sheeting down relentlessly. Above, a chunk of ceiling blasted out as if under the onslaught of a cannon, and through that hole came a stream of brown riverwater with the surge and focus of a fire hose, its force straining the hole until more ceiling gave way and the flow began to resemble that of a burst hydrant, with incredible

*force under which an entire section of ceiling crumbled,
sending water dumping itself into the tunnel with the fury of
a dam break. Roaring down the roadway, a brown tidal wave
rolled beneath a jackknifed milk tanker and strode inexorably toward the survivors, who were still huddled near the
collapsed midriver passage.*

*For the first time in the seventy years since this tunnel had
been forged through its bed, the Hudson River had come
calling.*

LATONYA WASHINGTON

Before the flood start, we be sittin' on that high sidewalk,
me and Vincent and little Mikey. That rescue man, Latura,
he was talkin' to Officer Tyrell, takin' this funky vest back
from Tyrell and puttin' it on. Later I found out it was full
of explosives and shit.

Anyway, Mikey, he be shiverin' and cryin' and make me
feel sorry for him, make me think of Nordell, make me miss
my baby, so I put my arm around the little crackhead, hole
him to me.

"Hush now," I say. "You gone be fine. Don't you go
freakin' out on me, baby. We got places to go and people to
see."

Mikey, he be snifflin' and snufflin'. "We ain't gettin'
outta here."

"I don't wanna hear that shit. We got Mr. Rescue 911
with us now, don't we?"

But Mikey just shakin' his head and tears be rollin' down
his cheeks. Remember, 'sides bein' scared, he ain't had no
crack in some time.

"I didn't do nothin' so bad," he say. "I really didn't! I

never use no gun. All I ever did was steal a little, 'cause I had to. I never did nothin' so bad."

Vincent say, "What, you think we bein' punished? That what you think? Think we bein' sent to hell?"

"That exactly what I think," Mikey say. "God's doin' this to us. It's His fault."

Vincent just shake his head, laugh. I flash him a cold look. Then I squeeze Mikey's shoulder and say, "Don't be talkin' trash. We gone turn this around."

"How?" Mikey say, lookin' at me like I be crazy.

"We was on our way to a work farm, wasn't we? And that sucks, don't it?"

Mikey nods.

"Well, when we finally do get to that work farm, ain't gonna seem so bad."

Vincent laughs, say, "What a crock of shit!"

I throw him a look that would of made milk go bad.

Then, not wantin' to piss me off, Vincent change his tune. "Yeah, maybe she's right. Maybe they'll even reduce our sentence, after what we been through."

"Sure," I say. "'Fore you know it, we be chillin' back out on the street. Breakin' out the Miller tallboys, laughin' about this shit. Sellin' our stories to the paper, sittin' on *Oprah* talkin' about our 'brave ordeal.' "

"Yeah. We gone be famous," Mikey say, not cryin' no more, even smilin' a little.

But what I say get Vincent thinkin'. Now he look like *he* gone to cry, only I know he won't, 'cause that ain't macho.

He say, "Never knew how good I had it."

Tell you the truth, I didn't know if we ever gone get out of there. And I ain't really thinkin' about malt liquor and cigarettes. I be thinkin' about my sweet baby Nordell and how much my heart hurt, knowin' maybe I ain't never gone see him again.

But I don't show them that. And Mikey is smilin', thinkin' about bein' on TV, and Vincent see what I done with the kid, usin' psychology and shit, and look at me and smile and shake his head.

So I give Mikey the high five, and he be smilin' and laughin', and Vincent, he high-five me and we laughin' like crazy.

Only not for long.

Not when this sound like Niagara fuckin' Falls is comin' down the tunnel at us.

MADELYNE THOMPSON

Water came sheeting down toward us, and we all hopped up onto the sidewalk, any of us who weren't up there already, and at first it wasn't that deep, just a layer of it covering the roadway, but the awful roaring, an echoing roar like the devil turned on the tap water, simply scared the shit out of me.

The fourteen-year-old girl, Ashley, was huddling with her parents. She wasn't taping this; she was too frightened, and any vestige of snotty teenage demeanor was getting washed away with the dingy brown tide.

When the water came lapping up over the elevated sidewalk, the youngest of the street kids, Mikey, panicked big time.

He jumped off, with Latonya reaching out for him but not stopping him, and he started running toward the Manhattan end, screaming, "I ain't gonna drown! I ain't gonna drown!"

Officer Tyrell stepped down off the sidewalk—the guardrail was gone along there—and intercepted the boy, grabbing him by the arm. The kid tried to squirm free, but Tyrell stood his ground.

"No!" he said. Tyrell's voice was commanding and echoed

above the rush of water. The boy stopped squirming, and Tyrell spoke loud enough for everyone to hear. "This tube runs downhill. The Manhattan end's going to fill up first!"

Latura stepped down into the water and faced Tyrell, who still held on to Vincent. He pointed to a tunnel section up ahead, in the direction the water was flowing from, where smashed cars had come together in a grotesque accidental wall-to-wall dam.

"We've got to go that way," Latura said softly, but we could all hear him.

Steven Crighton, who'd been between his wife and daughter with an arm around both, stepped forward, and splashed down into the water up to the men. Mikey scrambled back up on the sidewalk next to Latonya, who brought him close to her with a motherly arm.

Crighton's eyes were wide; at first I thought he was hysterical, and there was surely some fear in there, but mostly it was indignation, as his tone displayed.

"What the hell are you talking about?" he demanded of Latura. "You want us to go *toward* the flooding? Are you *high*?"

"No, but we need to be. We need to get up on top of those piled-up cars."

Tyrell thought about that, and nodded. "He's right, Mr. Crighton. That's our best shot, at the moment."

"Come on, everybody!" Latura called, and waved us down from the elevated sidewalk. We couldn't walk along it because it was blocked with rubble from where the gas main blew the wall apart.

Then Latura was leading us, a shepherd with ten reluctant sheep, up the roadway as water sheeted toward us, over our shoes, our ankles, and it was cold, terribly cold. Teeth were chattering. Arms were folded. Husbands cradled wives, Latonya cradled Mikey. I walked just behind Latura, next to Tyrell.

"Shit, man!" Latonya said. "This water's freezin'!"

Latura glanced back at her, shrugged with his eyebrows. "We're at the bottom of the Hudson River. It's this cold even in the summer."

I heard somebody splashing next to me and Crighton had left his family behind to move up alongside Latura. Apparently he still was not entirely satisfied with this strategy.

"Look," Crighton said, "I'm going along with this because there's some logic behind it."

"Great," Latura said blandly.

"But let's get something straight. I have a fourteen-year-old daughter down here and her life means more to me than anything on earth."

"It should," Latura said flatly.

"So don't expect me to follow you blindly like this is the fucking military. I'm not going to cause you trouble, but I intend to raise questions. Do I make myself clear, Mr. Latura?"

"Crystal, Mr. Crighton."

Mollified, for the moment anyway, Crighton fell back in line with his family.

Eleanor Trilling, who was leading her dog along through the water, was right behind me.

"Latura," she was saying to her husband. "Latura . . . I know that name." Then she raised her voice so that Latura could hear: "Didn't I read about you in the papers?"

He didn't reply.

From behind us I heard Latonya say, "Yeah, he's some kind of hero and shit, right?"

"Well, no," Mrs. Trilling said. "Actually, no . . . I think it was some kind of scandal."

With the exception of Latura and Tyrell, the entire group

stopped in its tracks, and with no apparent sarcasm, Mrs. Trilling called out: "Or was that some other Latura? Someone else who worked for the city rescue department?"

Now Latura stopped, and so did Tyrell. But the water didn't. It rolled resolutely over our ankles, chilling us. Not any more than Mrs. Trilling's words, however.

"What kind of scandal?" Crighton, moving up again, was asking Mrs. Trilling, but his eyes were on Latura, who, though stopped, still had his back to us.

"Not the kind that matters in here," Latura said, without looking at us. "Let's press on, people. . . ."

"It matters to Mrs. Trilling and myself," Roger said. "It matters very much indeed."

All eyes were on Mrs. Trilling, who shrugged and said, "I don't remember the details. He was . . . chief of something. Some people lost their lives and he was involved. I'm sorry, but that's all I remember."

"I read about it, too," Sarah Crighton said; the blood had drained from her face, but in this light, she looked a sickly brownish green. "You were *indicted,* weren't you?"

He turned and looked at our sorry little group. His face was blank, but his eyes were sorrowful.

"I took responsibility," he said.

I felt anger rising. Here he was, trying to save our asses, risking his own, and they're attacking him!

Crighton was saying, "Oh, great, oh fine. *That's* who the city sends down to help us! A fucking screwup! Some clown who got people killed!"

"That's enough," I said, grabbing Crighton by the arm. It startled him. I let go and continued. "Why don't you people take a good hard look at yourself in this muddy mirror at our feet? This man volunteered to come down here to help us. So lay the hell off. His past is *his past*. If you don't want to follow him, don't follow him! Swim down to Manhattan and drown and let the rest of us try to survive!''

For a few seconds the only sound was the rush of water at our feet. Latura's expression stayed blank, but his eyes seemed to smile, just a little, as he gazed at me.

''She's right,'' Mrs. Trilling said. ''Mr. Latura, please accept my apology. That was quite rude.''

''Rude?'' Crighton said. ''Rude? Are you joking? This isn't some goddamn country-club outing. Don't speak for *me*, lady. I have a *child* down here!''

Mrs. Trilling was visibly hurt by that remark as she drew her precious Cooper to her. ''Our family is as precious to us, Mr. Crighton, as yours is to you.''

''Well, pardon me if I make my daughter's life a higher priority than your damn dog.'' Crighton turned to me and said bitterly, ''This man's past may well have a great deal to do with our future. We're going to drown down here, and if he's all we've got—''

''If you agree that I'm all you've got,'' Latura said calmly, ''why don't you meet me halfway?''

''What do you mean?'' Crighton asked.

''Let me give you the opportunity to help yourselves.''

Latura was so unargumentative about it that the steam went out of Crighton's posturing. He could only say, ''Well . . . fine. I'm listening. We're all listening.''

''Steven . . . you mind if I call you Steven, or is it Steve? This 'mister' and 'missus' stuff is for strangers, and we can't afford to be that, anymore.''

''Fine. Fine. Steven.''

''My friends call me Kit. Now, Steven, I'm glad you brought that up—drowning, I mean—because I have good news and I have bad news on that score. Good news is, there's still time to stop that leak before it gets high enough in here to drown us.''

''And the bad news?'' Crighton asked, somewhat smugly.

"The bad news is the temperature of this water, which several of you have already noted."

"It's fuckin' *cold,* man!" Latonya hollered out.

"Exactly," Latura said, with a tiny smile, but that smile vanished as he said, "This water's at about thirty-eight degrees, at the moment. You don't have to worry about drowning in water that cold—the hypothermia would take you out long before that."

Vincent asked, "Hypo-what?"

"Thermia. Hypothermia," Latura said.

"Your body loses its inner heat," I said hollowly, "and shuts down."

Latura nodded. "You feel like you're getting tired, but you're actually getting dead. Now, I don't mean to alarm you, but you need the facts. And another fact is, we can't stand here yammering about this without wasting valuable time. Agreed?"

There were a few sighs, but mostly nods all around; finally, even Crighton nodded.

"Now," Latura said, beginning to walk again as we all trailed splish-splashingly along, "hypothermia's not going to get any of us, because we're going to look out for each other. And we're going to stay high and dry on top of that car dam."

Soon we were there, where the crashed-together cars, some of them three deep, formed a blockade, holding back the flow of the water somewhat. We tried not to look too close— some of the cars were burned shells with charred corpses inside, while others had flipped over on their collapsed roofs, and though we couldn't see them, we knew the crushed bodies of their occupants were within. The wall of mangled metal that was providing us with higher ground was at the expense of these unfortunate dead, and the atmosphere this shared knowledge created was as chilling as the water we fled as we helped each other up there.

From this vantage point, we could see a milk tanker jack-knifed across the roadway, forty feet from the oncoming deluge, which (like our car dam) was also slowing it, damming it, somewhat. Beyond the deluge, through the wall of water streaming from the ceiling, could be made out the orange and yellow and blue of the unremitting toxic fire as it burned, and the billowing black smoke it produced.

Everyone found a flat area to stake out on the "roof" of the car dam. The Crightons made their little space, and Mikey was sitting with the Trillings, petting Cooper. Latonya was staying near me, and I was, frankly, staying near the man I saw as our best bet: Kit Latura. Officer Tyrell stayed near Latura, too. Vincent was keeping to himself.

Finally, Steven Crighton said, "Okay. Now we're up here. High and dry. *Now* what?"

Latura was checking the various items in the pockets of his vest. "Now I'm going to collapse a section of the tunnel," he said. "That is, this north tube we're in. That should seal us off from the fire and plug the leak."

"What do you mean, 'seal it off'?" Crighton asked edgily. "Collapse it how?"

"By an explosion."

Crighton threw his arms in the air, wide eyes searching the ceiling. "*That's* your plan! Another explosion, down here?" Now he looked pointedly at Latura. "Are you completely out of your mind? Is this sort of thinking how you got those *other* people killed?"

Latura stayed calm, kept checking those pockets. Very evenly he said, "If you have a better idea, Steven, I'm open to suggestions."

"Of course I don't have a 'better idea'! That's not the point—"

"It's precisely the point," Latura said, clipping off the words. "We have a limited amount of time. We don't have the luxury of breaking up into discussion groups."

Latura raised his voice so that all could hear him over the ongoing rush of water.

"You people have to decide, *right now,* whether you trust me or not. And if you can make that leap of faith, you have to be willing to help me. Not blindly, but we have to be a team, we have to work together. Are you up for that?"

I nodded, but the others were just exchanging wary looks.

"Understand something, please," Latura said. "If we don't keep jumping from one chunk of the ice floe to another, we're goin' over the falls! Do you follow that? Are you with me?"

Again they exchanged glances, but now the nods followed; even Steven Crighton nodded, even he knew that however uncertain he might be about Kit Latura, the man was making sense. And who else had a better idea, *any* idea? Who else had any relevant expertise?

Nobody.

"Now"—Latura sighed—"I need somebody to go up to the Manhattan end of the tunnel, to see if they're making any progress. Steven, how about you?"

Suddenly Crighton's demeanor shifted; his indignation was replaced by blank apprehension.

"I've got a family here," he said. "I don't want to desert them."

His wife looked at him with disgust. "You're all talk, Steven. You always have been. . . ."

"Mom," Ashley said, trying not to give in to her own fear, her camera forgotten for the moment, though still attached to her hand like an extended appendage, "please don't. . . ."

The brown water streamed faster and faster, rising, higher, higher, gushing around the dam of cars.

"I'll go," Tyrell said. "It's my job to go."

Latura nodded at him, then studied him. "Is your first name George?"

"Yeah," Tyrell said, grinning. "How'd you know that?"

"Friend of yours named Grace asked me to give you a message."

Tyrell's grin turned melancholy. "Yeah?"

"She says she wants her damn bracelet back."

"Ha! With pleasure."

Latura helped Tyrell lower himself into the now knee-deep water and we watched his solitary figure get smaller as he trudged off, slogging toward Manhattan.

"Now," Latura said, turning toward the rest of us. "Who wants to give me a hand down by that milk truck, setting these explosives?"

He looked at Crighton, who just looked away.

Then he turned to me. "How about you?"

"Who, me?"

He gave me half a smile; his eyes were bright and lively under their hoods. "Weren't you the young lady handling that live wire before?"

"Sure, but—"

"Well, this wire won't be bucking like a bronco. I just need a steady hand, cool head, and a keen eye."

"I don't know. . . ."

"Come on, live wire. You're our cable guy." He offered his hand. "Ready?"

Then I laughed. I don't know why. Nervous laugh, I guess.

"Ready," I said.

9

MILK RUN

Under arc lights that turned night to day, EMS technicians with picks and shovels and ropes were making incremental progress at the rock pile where mere hours before the Manhattan entrance to the tunnel had stood. Wherever the remaining structure had allowed, seismographs had been strapped, guiding the rescue workers as they made their slow, painstaking, dangerous way into the collapsed entry area, hoping to find even one survivor trapped in a not-quite-squashed car or an air pocket. These methodical efforts clearly would not help any survivors deeper within the tunnel.

Out on the Hudson, searchlights played over icy black waters, as Coast Guard cutters and Harbor Rescue craft trolled, using sonar devices, listening for any sound of life in the tunnel far below.

They heard nothing.

Their reports were not heartening to those in the still-bustling, buzzing control room. Even more crowded now, the interweave of cubbyholes included engineers and Emergency Rescue chiefs from other cities, huddling in groups, expressing their thoughts, opinions, and facts in staccato rhythms appropriate to their knowledge of the dwindling time factor.

GRACE LINCOLN

I had all the rescue units in the field patched through my console. Deputy Chief Kraft and Norm, and Boom, too, were bunched around me, waiting, praying for something positive.

"Still not getting any trace of them," I said.

Norm sighed, shook his head. "We're going to have to take the gloves off, and start tearing that damn thing open from the Manhattan side."

I frowned. "Whose idea is that?"

Norm gestured around him, where the experts were gathered in intense little groups. "That's what they're all telling me. Seems to be the consensus."

"Consensus, my ass!" Boom exploded. "That tube is sealed like a goddamn lightbulb—a sudden shift in pressure, and it'll go *pop*!"

Kraft's expression was grave. "If there's anybody left alive in there, clearing the Manhattan side is their only hope."

"Give it a little more time, Chief," I said. "Maybe we'll hear something. . . ."

Norm was shaking his head reluctantly. "Grace, time is a commodity that's just too precious to gamble with at this point," he said. "I've heard from every expert in this room—"

"You haven't heard from Chief Latura," Boom said.

"That's right," Kraft said, firm but not unsympathetic, even though the reference to Latura as "Chief" was something of a slap. "And that means we're not *going* to."

Boom sneered at her boss, blatantly insolent. "You know what I think, *Chief* Kraft? I think you're a little too anxious to write Kit Latura off. Maybe you've got something *personal* to prove—"

"You're out of line, Dix," Kraft snapped. "Way the hell out of line!" He sighed heavily and shook his head. "I should never have let him go in without a plan."

"He *had* a plan!" Boom said.

"No. He had a way to get in, and a wild hair up his tail about sealing off the fire, but it was a long shot I shouldn't have allowed him to play. Because once in, he didn't have a way *out* figured, did he?"

That silenced Boom.

Kraft had a point. That was Latura's style: one step at a time, one problem solved at a time; but even with that notorious black mark on his record, Latura's reputation among those in the know was that of somebody who'd pulled off some pretty remarkable rescues.

"Whether you respect me or not," Kraft said to Boom quietly, "I respect you. I need your input on the best, quickest, safest way to open that seal."

Boom took that like a blow to the solar plexus; but then she heaved a long sigh, and nodded.

Norm said to me, "Grace, a word in private?"

"Sure," I said, and we headed over to his glassed-in office while Boom and her deputy chief were confabbing about this latest problem under a tentative white flag.

Norm shut his office door and said, awkwardly smiling, "You know, I never have run that tight a ship."

"You've always been a great boss, Norm. Easy to work for. So what's this about? I am a little busy."

He was clearly embarrassed. "I, uh . . . know you and George Tyrell have been seeing each other."

"Norm, I—"

He raised a hand to gently stop me. "I knew it violated departmental fraternization policy, but I just didn't give a shit. I figure your personal business is your personal business."

"Thanks, Norm."

"Since George is down there, I've decided to share this decision with you. Because, let's face it—who am I trying to kid? Everybody around here knows who *really* runs this place."

I could only smile. "That's sweet, Norm."

His expression was firm, but his eyes were frustrated. "I believe we've got to unseal that tube at the Manhattan end. With whatever it takes."

"You really think that's our best shot? You think the tube can withstand that? The pressure shifts . . . ?"

He shrugged. "Nobody knows. Is it our best shot? By default, maybe. Hell, everything's a guess, a gamble. But the worst thing we could do now would be sit here on our asses, and do *nothing*."

He was right.

"Okay, then," I said. "You want my blessing, you got it."

"You're with me?"

I swallowed and nodded glumly. "Open it up."

MADELYNE THOMPSON

So there we were, Kit Latura and I, slogging in knee-deep freezing water, moving toward the leak cascading from the ceiling of the tunnel.

He glanced over as we sloshed in step. "You mind if I ask you a personal question?"

"Not at this point."

"What's your name?"

I laughed. "I guess it never came up before, even though you were lying on top of me. . . . It's Madelyne. Madelyne Thompson."

"Madelyne," he said, as if savoring it. "That's a good old-fashioned name."

"What kind of name is Kit?"

"Didn't you ever hear of Kit Carson?"

"Sure. Western hero."

"Also an old TV show. My mom had a crush on the actor."

"Hey, my best friend was named after a soap-opera character. How would you like to go through life called Kayla?"

He grinned, shrugged. "I've lived with Kit. I figure if I can survive that, I can survive a little water. . . . Madelyne, thanks for what you said back there."

"No thanks necessary."

"You're doing good. Handle yourself well."

"Doing good? Handle myself well? Try 'scared shitless'!"

"Who isn't? But you're dealing with it."

We kept plowing through the icy water; my teeth were chattering.

"The way you handled that cable," he said, "not everyone could've done that."

"Wasn't much of a choice."

"Sure there's a choice. It's like the first guy that ate a raw oyster."

"What are you talking about?"

He shrugged. "Don't you figure that guy must've been on his last legs? Starving to death or something? You know, to even get involved with a raw oyster. Don't you figure he was faced with, I eat this, or I die. I mean, it's slimy, looks like something you coughed up. Then there's this little moment of truth before he sucks that little slider down. How did he have the courage to try it? I'll tell ya how—he had the will to survive. He dug down deep and found it inside himself. Like you did.''

''I'm going to take that as a compliment.''

''That's how it's meant. You're not a native New Yorker, are ya?''

''Not hardly. Strictly Midwest. Is idle chatter supposed to calm down borderline hysterics? Are you using some technique on me you learned somewhere?''

God, the water was cold.

''Maybe,'' he said. ''Where in the Midwest?''

''LaPorte, Indiana. I went to the University of Iowa... the Writers Workshop?''

''So you're a writer?''

''Playwright.''

''That's how you wound up in New York?''

''Yeah. Trying to get my plays produced.''

''Any luck?''

''No. Funny.'' And I actually laughed; it echoed off the rounded ceiling and was punctuated by our sloshing footsteps. ''I was heading back home. Got fed up with the 'quality of life' here in the Big Apple.''

''Gettin' plays produced,'' he said. ''I hear that's a pretty tough thing to do.''

''Yeah,'' I said. ''Kind of the literary equivalent of trying to find your way out of a caved-in tunnel at the bottom of the Hudson River.''

A burst of fire from the nearby elevated sidewalk, a belated chain reaction from the gas-main explosion, put an exclamation point at the end of my sentence—and startled the hell out of me, and I lost my footing.

Latura grabbed me, sheltered me in his arms—from the tongue of flame—and then when it receded, we were in an awkward embrace that we quickly released.

Then we continued slogging through the cold brown water. After a while we came upon another dam of cars, not as substantial as the one our little group was camped on back behind us, but blocking the entire roadway nonetheless. As he helped me up and over it, we talked.

"Do we really have a chance?" I asked.

"Most definitely."

"You can tell me the truth. I can take it . . . I think. Anyway, I want to know. Got to know . . . Are we really getting out of this?"

"Of course we are," he said, almost casually. Then he grinned a little. "You got plays to write, don't you?"

Before long we'd made it to the overturned milk truck, its shiny sheet-metal tank extending across both lanes of the roadbed. Water raced beneath its wheels like a sierra stream. Above the capsized truck, where the ceiling had given way, loomed the exposed structural arches of the curved tube itself. At either end of the truck, welded-on ladders followed the curve of its tank, and Latura started up one of them, and I followed his lead, scaling the other.

Then we were standing on the rounded surface of the truck, the "top" of it (actually, one side of it), and a thumping sound caught my attention. I glanced down and a car that had crashed into the wall over the sidewalk had its back end in the rising water, and a male corpse was trapped in its shattered back windshield, water pressure knocking his arms on the car's trunk as if he were a sodden rag doll.

"My God," I gasped.

Latura was next to me, his hand on my arm. He said, very

calmly, "Keep your eye on the ball, Madelyne. Our world, right now, is on top of this tanker, and along that ceiling ledge, there. This is where we have to seal this baby up. Understand?"

I nodded.

He showed me a small glass vial from one of the many pockets of that funky vest.

"This is lead azide," he said. "Now, I'm going to briefly explain what we have to do. . . ."

And he did. I did my best to absorb it all, and only asked one question.

Then he was handing me a spool of copper wire, taking the loose end of it, then hoisting himself up onto the ledge of the broken ceiling, an area he could crawl along like a cat.

Fifty feet away was the crack in the cast-iron tube from which murky brown riverwater cascaded, tearing through the breach, placing terrible pressure on the other ancient iron sections. After seventy years they had to be rusted, rotten even, and they were slowly peeling back, the rift widening.

This was where Kit Latura was edging toward, and the ledge of the ruined ceiling got larger toward that terrible showering breach, forming a sort of small peninsula that gave him more room to work. I could see him carefully removing a vial from his vest, and he was about to set it in its small detonating case when a screeching metallic roar signaled that something was very wrong.

I gasped as Latura dove back along the narrow ledge, and a section of the tube itself came ripping out, a segment of cast-iron ring crashing down, shearing off the ceiling fragment he'd been crouching on, taking it down into the water, where both made a splash like a diving whale.

"Kit! Kit!" I called.

I could see him, on his stomach, on the ledge, the vial

dangling precariously from his fingertips. Shit, was he unconscious? And if he dropped that vial of explosive, would we both be blown to pieces?

But suddenly he was looking up, pushing up on one hand, and even at this distance I could see his silly little smile.

"You makin' mental notes, Madelyne?" he shouted over the deafening roar of water.

"Oh, yeah!"

"This might make a good play! Not a dry seat in the house!"

My laugh had some hysteria in it. "Yes—yes! I'm getting it all down!"

"Good! 'Cause the first thing I'm going to do when we get outta here, is forget it!"

And he got back to work.

I could see him slipping the vial oh so carefully into its detonating case, attaching the wires. . . .

"Good, good," I said to myself.

Then, with the vial clenched in his teeth, he jumped up and caught the edge of where the tube had given way; water was crashing down next to him as he raised himself smoothly up in a one-handed pull-up, using his other hand to dig away mud—part of the riverbed itself!—from around the exposed section of cast-iron tubing, making a space for the explosive, which he tucked as far back underneath as he could manage, packing it in with mud.

Then he dropped back down on the ceiling ledge, and crawled back as quickly as he could.

And, miraculously, there he was, next to me on top of our milk truck, reaching out and taking the spool of wire from me. Then he withdrew a sort of pistol grip from his vest, its male plugs fitting snugly, perfectly, into two females set in the outer part of the spool of wire.

"We're hot," he said.

"That water's coming down awful hard back there."

"I know. If it keeps eroding the riverbed where I got the charge shielded, we could have a problem."

"You mean if it takes out that explosive you set?"

"Yeah. If that azide washes out, the only two options aren't wonderful."

"What are they?"

"The inside of the tunnel blows, or it doesn't blow at all."

"And either way we die?"

"Either way we die. You said you wanted the truth."

"Thank you for that. What are we waiting for, then?"

"Not a thing," he said. "In fact, we're outta here!"

And he nudged me toward my ladder, and soon I'd launched myself back into the current, and shit! It was waist-high now! There was a section of elevated sidewalk still intact, and I scrambled up onto that, which put the water back at ankle level.

Latura had come down that other ladder and was in the water, his back to me as he unspooled the wire, keeping an eye on where the water was rushing down beside his buried explosive.

I heard crumbling and snapping, and looked back, and the rusted bolts of the tubing had given way, the section starting to bend back.

"Fuck!"

That was the first time I'd heard Latura use the word, and I looked at him with alarm.

Which is how he was looking at the spool of wire in his hands: it had jammed.

"I got no time to fix this snag!" he yelled back at me. "Go. Go! Go! Go!"

But I wasn't going; I was frozen there on the elevated sidewalk. "You're too close!"

"Madelyne, there's no time for discussion. Go, *now*!"

Our eyes locked briefly, then I nodded, and took off as fast as I could, but running in water, and looking back to see how Latura was doing, definitely impeded my progress.

I was at that less substantial dam of cars when I looked back and saw that he had himself positioned with legs spread as he raised that pistol-grip detonator and held it at arm's length and fired.

He dropped the detonator into the water and turned to run in the waist-high stuff when the explosion tore into the riverbed; its thunderous roar was how you'd think an erupting volcano would sound.

Latura dove under the water and shock waves rolled over its surface, rippling it.

I got slammed back into the wall of dammed cars, getting the wind knocked out of me, and hung on to a car door, half crouching, gasping, trying to stay up out of the water, which was rolling toward me in surf's-up waves.

When I looked up, and looked toward where I'd last seen Latura dive under the water, I at first saw nothing, then there he was, closer to me, but not at all close, standing, facing me, panting for breath, spotting me, smiling.

But I wasn't smiling, not hardly, and he noticed that, and immediately looked behind him and saw where my dismay had arisen.

At the breach, the riverbed was pouring down into the tunnel, a mudslide of monumental proportions, hundreds of tons of muck, rock, and ooze, collapsing in, in seconds!

That was good, that was what Latura had intended.

But he had not figured that this mudslide would knock the milk truck over like a toy, ripping the tank off its brackets and—shit! The goddamn tank ripped off its brackets and began rolling down the tunnel like a chrome-plated steamroller . . .

. . . with Kit right in its path.

I began to scream, as if he needed any incentive, as if hysterical cheerleading would aid him in an insane, impossible race; but no problem could stop that son of a bitch. He was up and running, doing a hundred-yard sprint in waist-high mucky water, pursued by an eight-foot-high, eighteen-foot-long tank filled with milk.

And in moments it was bearing right down on him.

I wanted to look away, but I couldn't. It was coming toward me, too, but time had slowed down, the world was in an awful slow motion and yet going so terribly fast, and I hadn't thought of myself yet, just Kit, as the tank rolled over him.

"God, no!" I heard somebody say.

Me.

But when the tube rolled back around, I could see him! The crushing weight of the rolling tube had been offset, slightly, by those welded-on steel ladders we'd climbed, and Kit had somehow tucked himself behind one of them.

Then he was rolling out and up, scrambling to his feet and riding that rolling tube like a demented logroller. He was looking around frantically, and then spotted something, the hanging broken grille of a vent, and he jumped for it, grabbed it, hanging from it as the big cylinder, a seam split now, white liquid splashing, rolled on.

"Yes!" I cried.

And now it was coming right toward me.

"No . . ." I said.

And I clambered up the side of the car dam, clawing my way up on doors, on hoods, on anything.

Only I fell and with an awful splash was down in that murky water, and that's where I was when the damn thing came smashing into the far car, near the elevated sidewalk, hurling itself around, smashing into the car dam, its ride finally ending on a car hood, two feet from my head.

I couldn't breathe as I watched the huge silver tube rock to a stop.

Latura came wading around the thing, looking for me, and grinned at me. "How you doing?"

"I have definitely outgrown my need for milk," I said.

Then he was helping me over the car dam, with its white-oozing milk-tank addition, and we were standing in the muddy water, both of us soaked, both of us freezing, both of us with teeth chattering like those plastic windup magic-store gag choppers.

"Here," he said, slipping an arm around me, guiding me, "let's sit by a cozy fire."

And he led me to where a fire was blazing, though not raging, on the nearby elevated sidewalk.

We gathered warmth there, for a moment.

I looked back to where we'd come from; listened to the Niagara Falls–like sound. We both noticed a big teddy bear, torn, floating like a little corpse, drifting by in the strong current.

I said, "The water's still coming in, isn't it? Even after the blast."

"Yeah. Yeah, it is."

"Hell."

"You asked for the truth. That's the truth."

"What did we accomplish?"

"It's not coming in as fast. We bought some time. A little time."

And we began to trudge through the water back toward the others.

10

WHAT COMES NEXT

At the Manhattan entrance, along the perimeter, a Red Sea of fire engines parted, and underscored by the throaty roar of heavy diesel, haloed in searchlights and other disaster-site illumination, appearing first as silhouetted steel monsters worthy of so fearsome a name, the bulldozerlike jackhammer-limbed Scorpions rolled toward the caved-in entry.

Emergency Rescue had set up its own center of operations here. Deputy Chief Frank Kraft crossed from the command triage to where the gleaming, ominous digging machines were moving into place.

I found the deputy chief watching those damn Scorpions rumble into position and I said, real casual, "Ever been in a hard-rock mine?"

He didn't look at me; his mouth twitched before he said, "Can't say as I have. What's that got to do with anything?"

"Get a cave-in at a hard-rock mine, the miners' families line up at the entrance. Carry candles. Wait for word. It's like this."

"We're not standing around praying," he said crisply. "We're *doing* something."

"Yeah. Signing a bunch of goddamn death warrants."

"Dammit, Boom!" His sigh was as weary as it was frustrated. "Seismo's just read a horrible explosion down there—"

"That's what the chief went down there to do! Set an explosion!"

He was shaking his head; he looked bad, eyes baggy, flesh all gray. "It's been seven hours," he said. "The air down there is poison. The tunnel's flooding. Face the truth, for Christ's sake! They're already dead."

The arms of those big metal bugs were extended, their titanium bits poised, dentist drills from hell.

"That's what the mining company always says," I told him, "right before they put the nail in the coffin. They just can't wait to get that mine reopened. After all, they can always find more miners to put inside."

"What the hell are you talking about? This is no goddamn mining company. Our job is to save lives here, and that's what we're doing."

But judging by his pained expression, I'm not so sure he was convincing himself any better than he was me.

ASHLEY CRIGHTON

After we heard the explosion, and everybody kind of took cover, we peeked out, from up on that fortress of crushed cars, and where, before, water had been streaming at us, getting higher and higher, it was like it had stopped.

I mean, there was still a lot of water down there, but it wasn't rushing at us. It wasn't rising, not that you could tell, anyway.

"He did it," I said. Then I hollered: "He *did* it!"

And suddenly Latonya and Vincent and Mikey and everybody, even the Trillings, were cheering and whooping, Cooper barking like he understood, too.

Mom slipped her arm around me. "We're going to be okay. We're going to make it."

"What makes you think so?" Daddy asked.

He was the only one who hadn't been cheering. He didn't like being wrong. I wonder if any father on the planet can admit being wrong.

"Steven," Mom said sternly.

"Somebody needs to ask the hard questions," Daddy said defensively. "Little details . . . like how the hell are we going to get out of here."

Mom slapped him. A hard slap that must have stung awful bad. His cheek turned bright red.

"Mom!" I yelled, grabbing her hand in case she was going to do it again. Daddy was behaving like an ass, but I didn't like seeing him slapped by her. Humiliated like that.

Even though I was restraining her, she got right in Daddy's face and screamed, "We're still here, aren't we?! We're still *alive,* aren't we?! Just once, Steven, *just once,* I wish you could stop tearing things down, and appreciate what you *do* have!''

He didn't say anything at first. I thought for a second he was going to cry. The only sounds were water drops pinging somewhere, like after a rain or down in a sewer.

"I do appreciate what I have," Daddy said, his whole face that bright color red now. "*My family.* That's why I'm fighting to keep it."

But he was looking at me, not Mom and me, when he said it.

MADELYNE THOMPSON

When we trudged back to the car dam, where the rest of our little group awaited, Latura and I received a warm welcome, or anyway as warm as possible considering the freezing water all around us. Steven Crighton was the only exception; he seemed sulky—maybe, on some idiotic level, he was resentful that Latura had succeeded, and made him look bad.

We'd barely arrived when, from the Manhattan end of the tunnel, splashing footsteps announced the return of Officer Tyrell. He was down there in the waist-high water, making his way back through the obstacle course of sunken cars.

"I heard machines!" he called to us, his voice echoing. "They're digging out the Manhattan end!"

"All right!" Latonya said, and everybody, even Steven Crighton, got bright-eyed and hopeful, handshakes, high fives, and hugs all around, and despite my chattering teeth and exhaustion from my little jaunt uptunnel with Latura, I felt a rush of joy and adrenaline . . . until I noticed Latura's glum countenance.

"What is it?" I asked him quietly. Almost whispering in the midst of all that joyful babble. "What's wrong? They're digging us out...."

"Pressure," he said.

"What?"

"They're not thinking about the pressure." He shrugged with his eyebrows. "Or maybe they are. Maybe they think we're all dead."

"They can't possibly—"

But a horrible, echoing cracking, like the vertebrae of God's spine shifting, ended all conversation as everyone of us turned toward the approaching Officer Tyrell. He stood motionless in the waist-high water with the expression of a man sneaking in, hoping not to waken a sleeping spouse, as behind him, a pickup loaded with charred lumber seemed to rise out of the water as if on a forklift. The echoing thunder cracks continued, and far faster than I can describe, the road-bed collapsed and Tyrell disappeared, swallowed under the murky water as a section of concrete behind him rose up, as if he were riding the wrong end of an immense teeter-totter.

Tyrell surfaced, swimming, anyway paddling, scrambling to stay above water when another huge chunk of roadbed rose in front of him and blocked him from our view.

Latura leaped from the car dam, but when he reached the water, he didn't swim, he ran, like a horse galloping down-stream, plowing through the water to get to where Tyrell was trapped at the base of a huge jagged concrete V.

I followed. No heroic leap for me; I climbed gingerly down the car dam and moved as quickly through the icy water as possible.

"What the hell happened?" I asked.

"Careful!" Latura said. Like me, only his upper torso was visible, the rest underwater. "I'm standing at the edge of the drop-off. Keep behind me.... Guess some undersection of the roadbed must not have been flooded, and the weight of the water got to be too much. . . ."

That pickup truck, a Datsun, was at the base of the V, too, and that was what had Tyrell pinned there—not the concrete itself. His neck was bent at a terrible angle. Water was rushing in from all sides around him, as if he were a bug caught in a drain under a relentless faucet.

Latura carefully stepped forward, edged his way down the crevice, into the V, next to Tyrell. With a paramedic's skilled swiftness, Latura checked him over.

"I can't feel my body," Tyrell said.

Latura put his back to the nose of the pickup, found a bumper to grab, and tried to lift it off. The biceps in his arms bulged mightily, but three of him couldn't have lifted that damn truck off Tyrell, not at that angle, anyway. It didn't budge.

"Oh God, oh God," Tyrell was moaning; then he caught a mouthful of water and began to splutter. The water was rising, and with his neck at that awful angle anyway, Tyrell was moments away from submersion.

"Hold on, big guy," Latura said. "Just a couple more seconds . . ."

Latura popped open the hood of the pickup, whipped a butterfly knife from one of his vest pockets, and sliced off a hose within, an air-conditioning hose, I think.

"Breathe through this," Latura said, and inserted the hose in Tyrell's mouth. "That's it, that's it—easy now."

I climbed down in there and held the hose high for him. Tyrell, his face half-covered with water, looked up at me with eyes brimming with terror.

"Try to stay calm," I told him, and gave him the best reassuring smile I could. "We're going to get you out of this."

Then, suddenly, everybody else was there, climbing down

into the water-swirling V. Only Ashley had not climbed down in, and she was nearby, too, taking footage on her video cam, capturing something remarkable: this disparate, at times contentious little group was working together. A team.

"Leverage!" Latura called out. "We need leverage!"

Steven Crighton and Roger Trilling threw charred wood off the load of the pickup, found a couple good two-by-fours, and quickly put them in position as levers.

"Ladies," Latura said, "be at the ready to pull Officer Tyrell out of harm's way. . . . Guys, let's put some muscle into it."

I turned the makeshift air hose over to Eleanor Trilling, and waited and watched as Steven, Roger, Vincent, and even little Mikey joined with Latura, backs to the pickup.

Latura led the charge: "One . . . two . . . *three*!"

And with one mighty collective push, they moved the pickup just far enough for Latonya and Sarah Crighton and me to slide Tyrell out from under.

"Hold his head steady!" Latura yelled.

I was doing that, even as water was swirling in on us in its drainlike fashion.

"We gotta make a stretcher," Latura said, yanking a plank from the pickup and slipping it under the injured Tyrell. He whipped his belt off and looped it around the board and Tyrell's forehead, cinching it tight, trying to minimize the movement of the tunnel cop's head.

"Everybody get around," Latura said, and we did, crouching, getting our hands under the plank. "Ready? Lift!"

And we hoisted the plank with Tyrell on it up to waist level, struggling against the oncoming rush of swirling water, which was nearly filling the pit by now, the uneven surface of the concrete beneath our feet, and we were slipping, sliding, spitting out water as the drain circled in on us, doing an awkward dance but all pitching in ("I got it!"; "Easy!"; "Right behind you!"; "Steady!") and somehow we made it up and out of there, onto more even terrain, keeping the flat-on-his-back tunnel cop above the waist-high water as we struggled back to the home base of our car dam. It was as if we were a procession of warriors carrying home one of our fallen brothers on his shield. Wet warriors, drenched warriors . . .

But water was better than blood.

By the time we got him back, Officer Tyrell, stretched out on his plank on the "roof" of the car dam, was shivering uncontrollably.

"Hypothermia?" I asked Latura, in a whisper.

He nodded. "Severe," he whispered back. Then, loud enough for everyone to hear, he said, "Go through these cars! See if there's anything dry—clothes, floor mats, *anything*!"

We fanned out, did our best. It was grisly work at times; the corpses, charred and otherwise, made troublesome company. I came back with a blanket I'd found in a backseat and Latura was kneeling over Tyrell, whose eyes hovered between fear and hopelessness.

Teeth chattering, the cop said, "Jesus, I'm cold . . . so cold. . . ."

"Hang on, buddy," Latura said.

"Somethin' . . . somethin' in my pocket. Shirt pocket."

Latura fished out a bracelet, sparkly stones in a gold setting—rhinestones, I figured—fairly tacky. But it had some special meaning to our fallen warrior.

"See . . . see that . . . Grace gets it," Tyrell said. "Tell her . . . tell her . . . I mi-mi-miss her already."

Latura took one of Tyrell's limp hands and pressed the bracelet within it. "*You* give it to her."

Then Sarah Crighton was there with a duffel bag and she

140

was ripping it open; I pitched in with her, spreading the clothing out over Tyrell, covering him up. Vincent appeared with another blanket and we bundled that on, too.

After delivering whatever they'd found, each searcher returned to the quest for "anything dry." Facing those trapped corpses was better than watching Officer Tyrell fight the hypothermia that was waiting to lay claim to us all.

GRACE LINCOLN

They didn't let us smoke in the control room and I was about to climb the walls. I've never been a heavy smoker, except when I'm nervous, in which case I can turn chain-smoker in an instant.

Anyway, I left the building and moved across the bustle of activity that was the New Jersey side Emergency Site Headquarters. News cams were capturing any movement, including me crossing the compound, but I ignored them, and questions reporters hurled at me, and even the glare of beams from hovering helicopters.

I found the quietest place I could along the riverbank and stared out at the dark, wide Hudson as police cruisers ferried back and forth. Beyond the waters, the towers of Manhattan kept an impassive watch. I sucked on my cigarette and gave the smoke a go at my lungs.

"Want a drink?"

It was Norm. I wasn't aware he'd followed me out; or had he been out here already? No matter. Right now my boss was handing me a bottle in a brown paper bag.

"It's good stuff," he said. "Twelve-year-old Glenlivet. As a rule, I don't drink on the job, but . . ."

I took it from him and had a nice swig; it burned going down, making the cigarette smoke seem cool by comparison.

Wiping the residue from my mouth, to which I returned my cigarette, I said, "That's enough for now. When George comes up, I intend to get good and loaded."

He chuckled. "I never knew you smoked."

"Nice to know I've kept a *few* secrets from you."

Then we both chuckled, albeit grimly.

I looked back out at the dark, wide river.

"You know, I've got a feeling he's okay," I said. "I really do."

I was hoping to hear him agree with me.

But he just took a sip from the bottle in the bag.

ASHLEY CRIGHTON

We had some quiet time, there on top of those cars. Mr. Latura was looking after Officer Tyrell, and nobody was even talking about what maybe we should do next.

Latonya Washington and I, it turned out, were almost the same age, even though she seemed lots older, at least till she came over and wanted to talk, all of a sudden.

Actually, she wanted a favor.

"Y'know, if we drown and shit," she said, "they probably gonna fin' your camera."

"I guess."

"So, like—could I say some stuff? Since it might be my last chance?"

"Okay."

So she got herself positioned, and I said, "Rolling," like they do when they make movies, and she gave a little speech.

"If anybody find this tape, could they show it to my mom? Her name is Easter Kincaid . . . I use my daddy's last name, but he be dead a long time, so anyway . . . She live at 684 East 129th Street and I jus' want her to know that I'm really sorry about dissin' her last week. . . . I know she say the things she say, meanin' the best for me . . . and I ain't mad that she ain't gonna take Nordell, 'cause I understan' she's got her own life and no room to spare, 'cause she still got four in the house already and two of my sister's kids . . . and anyway. Aw, forget it.''

Just when Latonya was losing interest, Mikey moved in front of my viewfinder.

"I got one last request," he said. He seemed a lot older now than earlier. "It's for Anthony Mason of the New York Knicks. Anthony, if you see this on the news or somethin', how 'bout you fade my name in your hair for the play-offs, which I know you gonna make. Name's Miguel, but Mikey's shorter, and that'd be fine. Do that for me, okay?''

Funny thing. Mikey's spirits were pretty good, really, and Latonya, who'd spent a lot of time up till now comforting him, seemed really blue. She curled up on her side, like a baby still inside its mother, and I think she was crying. But I didn't get close enough to her to see.

I hope I don't seem prejudiced saying this, but she scared me a little.

MADELYNE THOMPSON

I was sitting with Latura near Tyrell, who was resting, but not sleeping. Latura wouldn't let him, keeping a close eye on him, watching his rising chest, checking his pulse occasionally.

"You're very good at what you do," I said.

"Thanks," Latura said.

"Too good to get fired."

"I didn't get fired."

"Oh?"

143

"I resigned."

"Oh."

"There's a difference."

"Right. But . . . you got people killed. That's what Mrs. Trilling said. Sarah Crighton, too."

"That's a fact."

"It is?"

He nodded. "But the facts don't always add up to the truth. But you know that, don't you? If you're any kind of writer, you do."

I was thinking about that, when a sudden intense hissing caught everyone's immediate attention.

Down the way, where Latura and I had warmed ourselves by that sidewalk fire, water was lapping up, putting it out; in fact, the elevated sidewalk was no longer visible. The water had risen over it.

"That sidewalk was dry," Mikey said, "last time I looked!"

"Oh shit," Vincent said. "That means the water is comin' back in!"

No one said anything for a while. The enormity, the awfulness of that news, was sinking in to the accompaniment of the hiss of the water spitting out the sidewalk flames. We were cold, exhausted, shivering. We had pulled together in the crisis, to rescue Officer Tyrell; and now everyone was again a united front.

Staring at Kit Latura.

Steven Crighton's voice was quietly bitter as he said, "I thought you said you *stopped* it."

"I slowed it down," Latura said. "I never said I could stop it, never said I did stop it. I slowed it down."

"What *can* stop it?" Sarah Crighton asked, her face a mask of dismay.

"Nothing," Latura said.

More silence, as the group absorbed this news, but soon there was an explosion of indignation and fear, everyone talking over another, true panic setting in for the first time.

All at once Eleanor Trilling, clutching her beloved dog, said, "*Now* what can we do?" while Latonya had her hands on her hips and was saying, "What's this 'slowed it down' shit?" and Steven Crighton was shouting, "Well, now we can die a slow death! Thank you very much!"

Then somebody screamed, "*Shut the fuck up!*"

Some hysterical woman.

Me.

"Let *him* talk," I said, jerking a thumb toward Latura. "Let him *talk*!"

I must have scared them, because now their collective gaze was focused on me, not Latura, who hadn't yet picked up my cue.

So I rattled on: "We'd all be dead right now if it wasn't for him. So back the hell off, and leave him alone!" I swallowed, tried to regain my composure, my dignity, and then said to Latura in a voice that didn't hide my own anxiety, "What are we going to do?"

Steven Crighton said, "I have an idea. Let's blow something else up."

I went nose to nose with the pompous yuppie bastard. "You've got a real gift, don't you? For making the worst of a bad situation."

Somebody pulled me away from him, and I'll be damned if it wasn't his wife. Seemed this woman didn't like anybody else criticizing her husband.

"Steven wasn't talking to you," she said, biting off the words, fury raging in her eyes. Then she pointed to Latura. "He was talking to *him*."

Quietly, in a surprisingly confrontational manner, Steven

Crighton faced Latura and said, "It's over, right? We're finished, aren't we? Just tell us. We have a right to know."

And then every face, including mine, was turned toward the man who represented the only hope we had. Waiting for him to tell us if any hope remained.

"At EMS," he said, "this is how we look at problems. You're called to the scene of an auto accident, right? Some poor bastard's severed an artery in his leg. You tourniquet that wound. *Then* you worry about saving the leg. You take things in order. You take them one at a time. You just keep doing *what comes next*."

Ashley Crighton, at her mother's side, was crying, tears streaming down her pretty face. "Can you please get us out of here? Please just get us out of here. I don't want to be in here anymore. I don't want to die."

Both her parents enfolded the girl in their arms in one big hug; well, at least they were a family again.

Latura sighed, nodded; his tension, his frustration, which he'd carefully hidden from us, was showing.

"Let me see what I can come up with," he said, and climbed down off the car dam, on the milktruck, mudslide side, slipped back into the water, where he splashed some up into his face and shook it off.

"Focus," he said, and he began to trudge forward very slowly, looking. Cooper barked at him, but Latura paid no attention.

He was evaluating his options.

CATHY "BOOM" DIX, EMS

I had to pitch in, even though I didn't approve of the effort. It's like being a soldier—unless you're at the point of mutiny, and ready to face court-martial, you just grit your teeth and do your goddamn duty.

So I worked with the other demolition engineers at the caved-in mouth of the tunnel, while the two Scorpion drivers climbed down for a smoke or whatever. Finally the demo guy in charge gave the thumbs-up to the waiting drivers, who climbed up on their big ugly babies and turned on their ignitions.

The starter coils whined, but the engines didn't fire.

Neither of them.

Puzzled, the two drivers climbed down and checked their engines. One, frowning, said, "Goddamned starter cable's gone! Somebody yanked it out!"

The other one said, "Me, too!"

I was standing off to one side, of course, pleased by the delay but mystified about how it could have happened. Then I noticed Deputy Chief Kraft standing next to me. He had a funny little smile on his face, and a manila envelope in one hand; he handed the envelope to me.

"File these," he said.

Now, apparently somebody saw the deputy chief hand me that envelope, and there's been speculation that Kraft, who was seen around those Scorpions about the time the other demo experts were preparing the caved-in tunnel mouth, may have removed the Scorpion starter cables. And, you know, stuck them in that manila envelope and gave them to me to dispose of.

But when they asked the chief, later, what he was doing around those Scorpions, he said, "My job—checking out every detail . . . but I frankly didn't notice those starter cables were gone."

And when I was asked what was in that envelope the deputy chief was seen handing me, I had to admit I couldn't remember.

I mean, there was a lot going on around there that night.

Like the flurry of activity around the Scorpions, trying to get them up and running again.

MADELYNE THOMPSON

Latura wasn't gone very long; when he came back, his eyes were alive with hope. And that sent hope racing through my system again, let me tell you.

He climbed nimbly back up the car dam and settled down at the side of Officer Tyrell, who was awake, but barely.

"The bunk rooms, George," Latura said, kneeling by the tunnel cop, a hand gently resting against the man's shoulder. "When they were building this tunnel, the sandhogs had bunk rooms down here—for naps during the long shifts. Norm Bassett told me. Is there a way in?"

"Don't know . . . I don't know. . . ."

"I know you're hurting, but think . . . a doorway, maybe a ladder . . ."

Tyrell's eyes tightened. "A hatch."

"A hatch?"

"In . . . in a guard booth . . ."

"Which guard booth, George?"

"Number . . . number three."

"Which one is that?"

"We're . . . we're near it now. Nobody ever . . . ever opened it . . . off-limits."

Now it was Latura's eyes that tightened. "Not anymore."

"Careful . . . the older guys . . . used to say it . . . it led straight . . . straight to hell."

Latura winced at hearing that, but it wasn't enough to stop him. Weren't we in hell already?

Getting to his feet, Latura clicked on his flashlight and

sent its beam sabering down the tunnel, across the water, down toward the second car dam that the milk tank had become part of. Beyond that was the oozing mountain of mud he'd created with his explosion.

But the flashlight beam landed on the remains of a guard booth that was clearly marked "#3."

Latura turned to Steven Crighton and said, "Take care of everybody till I get back."

It was a nice piece of psychology, putting Crighton in charge.

Then Latura climbed back down the car dam and found his way to the elevated sidewalk, which, though flooded, obviously wasn't as deep as the roadbed itself, and moved quickly toward the guard booth.

Eleanor Trilling, hugging her dog while her husband hugged her, said, "Maybe he's found a way out."

"At least he's trying," her husband said. "Maybe he's close to finding a way."

"Maybe!" Sarah Crighton almost yelled. "Maybe this, maybe that!"

Great. Her pain-in-the-ass husband finally quiets down, and now she's launching a full-scale rave-out.

"He's going to have to do better than 'maybe,' " she said bitterly.

Her daughter, Ashley, was looking at her with dismay.

"It's your *job* to get us out of here!" Sarah screamed down the tunnel after Latura, who didn't turn to respond, just trudged onward, toward the shambles of the guard booth.

Latonya, who, after all, was about the same age as Sarah's daughter, stepped forward and said, with dignity that by this point came as no surprise to me, "He don't have no answers for you. He don't know if we're gonna live or die. He don't know if he's gonna live or die. All he knows is, he ain't gonna stop *tryin'* to live. He showed me that. If you open

149

your damn eyes, lady, you might see it, too.''

Sarah was trembling, teetering between rage and embarrassment.

Her husband slipped an arm around her. ''She's right, dear. But so are you—it's his job. . . . Let's let him do it.''

And we quietly awaited his return.

11

THE WAY TO DAYLIGHT

*New starter cables installed, the Scorpions belatedly fired up
and lowered their massive arms into position. Soon the thunder of dueling jackhammers shook the night as onlookers
covered their ears, whenever possible heading for the shelter
of a tent, as a dust storm filled the air, the Scorpions cleaving
the slabs of concrete into powder.*

*The thunderous pounding at the Manhattan mouth of the
tunnel reverberated down the tube and brought news to Kit
Latura of an arriving cavalry that would bring death, not
deliverance.*

Latura only redoubled his efforts.

*Within the flooded, partially collapsed guard booth, he
threw the desk chair to one side, shoved the desk splashingly
aside, fished below in the muddy water, peeled back a rug,
finding something the desk had rested on: storm cellarlike
access doors.*

He pulled them open, and beckoning him through the shimmery murky waters were stairs leading steeply down; his flashlight probed the space, and old waterproof fixtures reflected dimly through the water.

He didn't walk down those stairs, he caught a deep breath and dove down them, following the shaft of the staircase, swimming down into a small square crawl space, four feet by four feet.

Treading beneath the water, using his waterproof flashlight as his lantern, he could make out framed black-and-white photographs of the construction of the tunnel, sandhogs at work, fastened to the walls; he was swimming through a history of the tunnel.

More important, there was a door in there, a hatchway door with a big circular handle, like something out of an ancient submersible.

And air bubbles were seeping out from behind that door.

The wheel didn't seem to want to turn, even under all of Latura's considerable strength; but finally it gave in, began to turn, and then gave way, the entire hatchway door ripping off at its rusted antique hinges, never to be reshut.

And Latura whooshed through into a chamber built a few feet above the level of the roadway—still dry, but for the water that had just rushed in with him.

He gasped for breath, slapped and rubbed himself to increase circulation, and flashed his light around, taking in something that was not a bunkhouse for overworked sandhogs at all.

MADELYNE THOMPSON

The atmosphere, as we were waiting, was neither one of hope nor despair. A certain sober resignation had set in. Not resignation that we were going to die, exactly. More like a sense that we were going to live, or die trying—but that sounds like we were enthusiastic and that's not it at all.

You had to be there.

Sitting on top of that car dam. Waiting. Smoke drifting. The lingering smell of gas from that ruptured main. Water drips. Water rushing in. That awful jackhammering that kept echoing down the tunnel. And yet it all added up to a kind of deadly silence.

Most of us were grouped together, except for the Crightons, Mom and Dad and Ashley, sitting at the far end, quietly talking, soothing each other, even laughing a little occasionally, taking this final opportunity, I guess, to become a family again.

Eleanor and Roger Trilling sat with their dog, and we were all nearby as Roger gave Mikey some tips on how to pet the animal.

"You ever have a dog?" Roger asked the boy.

"Only if you count his girls," Vincent chimed in.

Mikey flipped Vincent the finger, but it was a good-natured exchange between the street kids.

Roger was scratching under Cooper's neck and the dog was loving it. "You never want to pet a dog by coming up over their eyes. They feel threatened. They think they're being attacked."

Mikey nodded, reached out, and started scratching Cooper under the chin. Roger was looking fondly at the boy, a bittersweet look I don't think I'll ever forget; thinking back, I realize he must have been thinking about his own son, his late son, about whom we would be soon hearing from his wife, who'd become something of a motormouth, all of a sudden.

"We were on our way to Colt's Neck, that's home for me," she was saying, babbling almost, like a lot of frightened people tend to do. "Have you ever been out that way?"

"No," I said.

Eleanor was stroking Cooper's back even as Mikey continued to fuss with the dog, who seemed used to getting this kind of attention.

"We took Cooper to see a specialist," she said. "We had to wait *six months* to get in. Can you imagine? A six-month wait to see a vet? But it was worth it. He was very helpful." She leaned forward conspiratorially and I could see her husband wince. "He told us that Cooper is having mood swings."

If her expression hadn't been so spookily earnest, I might have laughed. Instead I just croaked, "A dog with mood swings?"

She nodded, knowingly, patting her baby. "All animals do."

"Eleanor," Roger said, "let's not get into—"

"She *wants* to hear," Eleanor said, meaning me, but I didn't, really. She looked at me and smiled; it seemed a mildly demented smile. "My husband's embarrassed. I embarrass him. But I don't care. I happen to think there's more to life than the corporeal."

Mikey frowned and said to Roger, "Are you in the army?"

"No, son," he said, with a weary smile.

Eleanor was leaning closer to me, having determined I was the only one here capable of understanding her discourse. "I believe in a spiritual world, even if my husband doesn't. Oh, I don't claim to have the answers. But Roger doesn't even want to hear the *questions*."

This was getting awkward.

"Uh, well," I said, "not everybody agrees on these kind of things. . . ."

I looked toward her husband and his eyes were flashing me a sort of storm warning.

"Our son, Jonathan, went trekking in Nepal," she said. "He caught some sort of fever. Nothing could be done, so they said."

Her husband touched her arm. "Please, Eleanor . . ."

She smiled, but it was a sad, crazy smile, and she hugged Cooper to her, Mikey jumping back a little as the animal was withdrawn from his attentions.

"Two days after the funeral," she said, "this animal arrived in our backyard. Just showed up, as if he'd been dropped from the sky. It was no coincidence. I knew, instantly. I recognized something in his eyes."

Mikey blurted, "You don't think this dog is your *kid*?"

Eleanor didn't react; she just stroked Cooper. "Who can say? Do you know where *your* soul will go, after you die?"

Roger Trilling sat slumped, his expression devastated, his humiliation complete. But none of us were judging him. Maybe, in another circumstance, one of us might have laughed at his wife, out of cruelty, or nervousness.

But here in this tunnel, in this coffin of concrete, steel, and water, this sad sick woman's words hit just a little too close to home.

Nothing else was said for a long time, and then Latonya, who had been staring down at the murky water as it lapped steadily higher, higher, higher, a wet raid against our fortress, stood and said, "*Fuck* fear."

A few of us laughed.

The girl crossed to Ashley, her peer from another world. "Say it, girl. 'Fuck fear.' "

"I . . . I don't use that kind of language, at home."

"We ain't home. Mama and Papa, you say it, too. Come on! '*Fuck* fear!' "

And, one by one, we all got into it; a brazen, obscene

chant that even the weak tunnel cop joined, a mantra against death, ringing down the tunnel in defiance of the circumstances that were conspiring to kill us.

Latura must have thought we were nuts, hearing this as he approached; he was smiling a little, anyway.

"I've found dry ground," he said. "Everybody come on down, keep together . . . head over to that guard booth and wait for me. Madelyne, hang back and help me with George, okay?"

"Sure," I said.

The others helped each other down off the cars, and got up on the elevated sidewalk, sloshing through the ankle-deep water up there, dodging occasional twisted, smoking obstacles.

"You want me to help you carry him?" I asked Latura, who was kneeling beside Tyrell. He looked up, and in the blankness of his expression, in the soulful sorrow of his dark eyes, I knew the answer.

The echo of jackhammering was incessant, the tunnel itself seeming to shudder. Yet throughout, when we spoke, we didn't have to raise our voices; it was as if we were in a dreamlike state. Latura's conversation with Officer Tyrell was no exception.

Latura brushed some sweat beads off Tyrell's forehead. "How you doin'?"

"You . . . you know how I'm doin'."

"You got a broken neck, George."

"I know."

"The dry ground I found is a chamber through a flooded passage. I can't move you through there."

"And I . . . I guess I can't exactly swim it."

"No."

"Funny. I . . . I don't know why, but I'm not scared."

156

"I can't promise to come back for you. I can promise to try."

"We both know . . . that won't be necessary. You save the ones that . . . that can be saved. Get these people to daylight."

"I'll try."

"I know you will. . . . Take the bracelet."

Choking back tears, Latura took the gaudy thing from Tyrell's hand.

"Wish I could talk to her," he said, "just one . . . one more time. . . . Sweet Jesus, I wish . . ."

"I'll tell her."

The jackhammering seemed to increase in volume, as if they were getting closer, closer. Saviors who would destroy us.

"Find it," Tyrell said, urgency strengthening his voice. "The way to daylight. *Find it.*"

And he died. Right there. Right then. Even though his expression didn't change, his eyes remained open, and his body didn't move, I knew in that moment he was dead. It was like the daylight in his eyes had gone out.

Latura hung his head. Maybe he was, like me, saying a silent prayer.

Then he closed George Tyrell's eyes, covered him with a blanket, and helped me down the wall of cars.

Soon we were crowded within the flooded guard booth, grouped around the entry to the underwater stairwell. Everybody was shivering violently from the freezing water.

"It's a short swim," Latura said, gesturing with his flashlight in hand. "Follow me."

Sarah Crighton, all the shrewishness absent from her voice now, said gently, "Kit . . . what about Officer Tyrell? George?"

Latura shook his head, sadly.

The news hit everyone like a body blow.

Latura helped us recover, saying, "His last thoughts were with us. He wants us to find daylight. Let's not let him down."

Steven Crighton stepped forward, his face consumed with a puttylike blankness. "I've . . . I've been on your ass from the beginning. . . . No excuse for how badly I went about it, but believe it or not, I meant well."

"I know. There's no need—"

"Let me take the rear. Make sure everybody gets through. I'm a hell of a swimmer."

The two men exchanged glances that conveyed in a moment respect, forgiveness, acceptance.

And then all around us, the tunnel pulsated violently.

"Time to go," Latura said.

Roger Trilling held out his arms to his wife, who was awkwardly holding their dog in her arms, trying to keep him up and out of the water, though he was as soaked as the rest of us, and as cold.

"I'll hold on to Cooper, dear," he said. "He'll be fine. We'll all be fine. You'll see."

Mikey had been tagging along with the couple, probably more because of the dog than the Trillings themselves, but you could see Roger was fond of the kid.

"Would you help Mrs. Trilling across?" Roger asked the boy.

"Glad to," he said. "I'll be right beside you, lady."

"Ready?" Latura asked.

Everyone nodded as the rumbling in the tunnel encouraged haste.

And, with Latura in the lead, we one by one dove down the stairs.

12

HOLY PLACE

The survivors, like a school of fish, followed Kit Latura and his flashlight beam through the underwater passageway, emerging at the foot of a half flight of stairs that led up to a dry chamber that they had expected to be a bunkhouse. That was what Latura and the dying George Tyrell had discussed, after all.

But, as Latura's flashlight traced the walls of their new home, they found themselves in a very different sort of room: pews, a pipe organ, votive candles, peeling gilt wallpaper, and looming over an altar, a lifesize clay crucifix affixed to a riveted metal plate.

They were the sudden, soaked, shivering, stunned congregation of a chapel built so very long ago, for workers denied their day of rest.

Latura directed them to gather in groups of two and three, telling them to sit close together on the benchlike pews and share body heat, which his cold-quaking flock did, while he rustled around, seeing what was available.

He found several 1920s-era Coleman lanterns. Withdrawing waterproof magnesium matches from a vest pocket, he lighted the wicks, then handed the lanterns around.

And now that the little chapel was illuminated with an orange glow, the fact that one of their number was missing became readily apparent to another of them—the party to whom that MIA meant so very much.

ROGER TRILLING

I tried to hold on to him, I really did, I damn near died doing it; but Cooper panicked underwater, got away from me, started swimming back where we came from, and I just didn't have enough air to go after him. All I could do was swim forward.

And now as I sat near Eleanor on a pew in the little chapel where Latura had led us, with lanterns providing a dim midnight-service glow, she realized he was missing.

"Cooper? Roger, where's *Cooper*?"

But she was up and out of the pew, heading for that stairway down to the hatchway, before I could answer. I stopped her two steps down, pulling her back up.

"He started to struggle, dear," I said. "I . . . I just couldn't hold him."

She was shaking her head violently, saying, "No, no, no! . . . We've got to go back for him. Mr. Latura! You've got to help me go back for him!"

Latura said nothing.

I was holding on to her; she was squirming to get free, desperate to scramble down the stairs and dive back into that water and seek her "son."

As gently but firmly as I could, I said, "We can't, Eleanor. We just can't."

"I won't lose him *twice!*"

That was when, finally, I lost control. I wish I hadn't, because I know it hurt her. And I meant for my words to do her good, but I'm not convinced they did.

But I'd held it in for so long and, well, I erupted.

"He was just a goddamn *dog,* Eleanor! *Listen* to me! He wasn't Jonathan Cooper Trilling. Jonathan, our son, is dead."

I gestured to the boy, Mikey, sitting in a pew nearby.

"This," I said, "is a boy. A human boy. Cooper was a dog, and this is a boy, and let's not confuse the two any longer!"

She wasn't struggling anymore, but her face was contorted and her arms were folded close to her, as if she were trying to squeeze inside herself. "You don't understand. You *never* understood. . . ."

"I understand perfectly," I said. "You think I didn't feel the same pain as you, at the loss of our son? You think I don't feel it now? We buried our son, Eleanor. The worst thing that can happen to parents has already happened to us. But we're still alive. We are *alive,* and we have each other, and—"

"It's not enough," she said. "It's not the same. . . ."

"And it never will be." I put my hands on her arms. "But we have to make the best of what we have . . . because it's all we have."

She looked up at me and her eyes were overflowing with tears, her lips quivering; she looked like a child, and as distorted as her sorrow-racked features were, I could still see her, in there somewhere, the pretty little sensitive college girl I fell in love with, how many lifetimes ago?

"He's gone, Roger. Jonathan's gone. . . ."

"Not as long as we remember him," I said. "And that'll be forever. Now come on, come back . . . let's sit together, with that boy, and get near one of those lanterns. You're going to freeze to death. . . ."

She let me take her in my arms and I held her close. She felt so very cold, and limp as a rag doll.

"I do miss him so," she said.

"I know . . . I miss Jonathan, too."

"Yes, I miss Jonathan . . . but I mean our poor poochie. I miss him, you must allow me to miss him. Even if you're right, and he is just a dog . . . he was ours, and he didn't deserve to die like that."

"Nobody does, darling," I said.

And she swallowed and smiled and told me she loved me.

Like so many couples, we said that to each other now and then, maybe not as often as we used to, but often enough, certainly more than some couples who'd been married as long as we had. Only it had been a long time since those words meant something, and I told her the same thing.

"I'm tired," she said. "Sleepy."

"Come on. We'll sit. Warm each other."

And we did. I held her. She loved me. I loved her. In that chapel, in those moments, something had finally healed, or at least started to.

I'll always remember that.

MADELYNE THOMPSON

The jackhammering was rattling the chapel as we huddled in the pews, in little pockets, around the lanterns, like kids around campfires.

Latura and I had a lantern to ourselves. And, finally, a moment to ourselves.

"So, Kit—what's the story?"

He just looked at me.

"You're big on telling it like it is," I said. "You've given these people hope, taken us over one hurdle after another . . . but never false hope. Never bullshit. So tell me—no bullshit. Here in the chapel—make your confession. What's the story?"

He swallowed; the planes of his handsome yet lumpy features had a rough-hewn majesty in the light of the lantern. Maybe "majesty" is a little much. Beauty? No. Dignity. That's it.

His voice was prayerfully quiet. "We were called up to the South Bronx. Collapsed building. Middle of the night. Just a damn tenement, condemned property, that finally fell in on itself. Probably a shooting gallery. You know, drugs? What the hell, it wasn't important. Even a junkie's life is a life, right?"

I nodded.

He swallowed again. Sighed. "We were the first ones on the scene—EMS, I mean—and the book said it wasn't our turf, which some of my guys pointed out to me. Wait for the cops, they said, the fire department . . . let *them* handle it. Everybody in there's dead anyway, my boys said. But we didn't *know* that. I couldn't stand around, waiting for somebody else to show up, waiting to sort out jurisdiction, while people burned to death in there."

"Even if they were only junkies," I said softly.

"Yes. Even if they were . . . only I was wrong. Nothing in there but corpses. Nobody to save. So we headed back out . . . but, on the way, a gas main blew."

"Jesus . . ."

He rubbed a hand over his forehead, through his dark hair, as he stared into the past. "Three of my men were killed—instantly. Thank God for that much. My second in command, my best friend on the job, or anywhere for that matter . . . his brother was one of them.''

"I'm so sorry. . . ."

Tiny shrug of the eyes. "There was going to be an inquiry. Some political nonsense was going on around us, already—funding cuts, some grandstanding in the media and by the media. . . ."

"I vaguely remember," I said.

"Anyway, bullshit things had been affecting the department, so there were these fucking jackals just waiting to bring us down. Plus, wrongful-death suits from some of the families . . . a real mess. I figured the department could weather it better if somebody took the responsibility."

"You mean the blame."

"Whatever. Anyway, I resigned."

I didn't know what to say to him. Had he been right, risking the lives of his men just in case some junkies had survived the collapse of that building?

"I had two choices," he said. "Do nothing—or do something. And I could be wrong, or I could be right. I made my choice. I had to stand behind it."

"Would you and your guys have been heroes, if you'd been right? If you'd hauled some live junkies out of that building, and none of your people were any the worse the wear for the effort, would you have been commended? Would the media have sung your praises?"

"It wouldn't have made the want-ad section. Who would have cared?"

"You."

He shrugged.

"Is that why you came down here?" I asked.

"What do you mean?"

"To . . . prove something? Or were you seeking some kind of personal atonement?"

He laughed humorlessly. "No bullshit?"

"No bullshit."

"None of it ever crossed my mind."

The jackhammering seemed suddenly much louder, its horrible echo shaking the cramped chapel, showering us with a snowstorm of dust. Sitting snugly sheltered between her parents, Ashley Crighton began to freak out.

"The water!" she cried. "It's still *coming*!"

And it was.

It had crept through the hatchway and risen up the steps and was now lapping onto the floor of the chapel itself. Seemed wherever we fled, the water came after us. And we were losing the chase.

Roger Trilling said, "Ellie? Ellie!"

The alarm in his voice sent all our eyes his way. He sat with his wife lying unconscious in his arms.

Latura rushed over, checking her pulse.

Roger, backing off to make room for the paramedic-trained rescue worker, had the same expression his wife had worn when she discovered their dog was missing.

"She said she was sleepy," Roger said. "She *just* closed her eyes."

"Hypothermia," Latura said, and began trying to revive her. He stayed at it a good while, but the CPR took no effect. She did look asleep. Peacefully asleep. Her expression, so often tortured these past hours, was at last serene. Cold, shivering, the rest of us could hardly be blamed for a tinge of envy.

"I'm sorry," Latura said to Roger, and moved away from the corpse.

Roger held his wife tight and tears streamed down his cheeks. At first everyone moved away, giving him room; but then we began to move closer to him. The situation seemed to call for that. For a show of support. Of sympathy.

We weren't strangers, anymore. We were a family. Maybe we didn't always like each other, but what family does?

"Ellie," he was saying softly, "please wake up. Oh, please wake up. . . ."

We could feel the water coming up around our feet, our ankles. The flood moving in steadily now as the jackhammers pounded, pounded. . . .

"Oh Jesus!" Latonya screamed. *"Look!"*

The water, covering where the steps had been, was roiling, as if bubbling, boiling, something moving there, something black, some black *things*. . . .

Rats.

Every rat in New York except the one I'd killed in my apartment was swimming toward us, scrambling, crawling, clawing up out of the water, their wet fur and their beady eyes creating a glistening black invading army.

We were up on the pews, then, but soon so were they!

They were on everything, us included, and Latonya's shrill scream was bouncing off the walls: "Get 'em offa me! Get 'em *offa* me!"

I was kicking, stomping, as they went scurrying around us, and they weren't lingering, but seemed to be fleeing past us, as if the Pied Piper were up ahead and they had to catch up.

But Latonya, freaking as she was, was just standing there with the damn things crawling up the legs of her orange jumpsuit, and I stomped over there and started batting them off the girl. Steffi Graf had nothing on me.

Then the bulk of the black wet repugnant writhing army had moved past us in the pews and was wriggling up the altar, as if they were going to Jesus.

And, damn, they *were*!

They were squirming their way up our Lord and Savior's crucified body, covering him as if taking rodent Communion, then up past his wounds, toward his pained compassionate countenance, and as if Jesus had performed the miracle himself, their number began to lessen as they reached the crown of thorns.

Soon only the upper half of Christ's torso wore a rat coat, then his neck and face, and unbelievably, the horde of the awful creatures was gone.

With the exception of a few stragglers up on the altar, the only rats in the chapel now were squashed, stomped dead ones, floating in the rising water.

"Little bastards," Vincent said, "deserting a sinking ship!"

"That's exactly what they're doing," Latura said, tightly, but with something approaching glee in his voice. He'd made his way to the crucifix, unbothered by the rats. "Look at this!"

Stepping from pew to pew, we made it to the altar, and gathered around, as if receiving some benediction from our EMS savior. He was pointing to the crucifix, or actually to a place in the metal plate the crucifix was fastened to, a rusted-out hole, a wide corrosion point in the metal.

And a few straggling rats were scampering up the Lord and into the rusted-out hole toward salvation.

Latura began pounding a fist on the plate and his pounding resounded hollowly.

"Those little bastards," Latura said, "know the way *out*."

The slam of jackhammering was sending tremors through the chapel.

"We're going to pry this thing out of the wall," Latura said, nodding toward Jesus.

Vincent moved forward, saying, "Mikey! Come on, man!"

And everybody pitched in, except the shellshocked Roger Trilling, who held his wife in his arms like a husband about to carry a bride across a threshold, and Latonya, who stood on a pew, shivering, not wanting to go anywhere near where those rats had gone to.

Latura leaped up and grabbed one of Christ's outstretched, forgiving arms, and pulled, making the crucifix strain at the corroded rivets of the metal plate; the rest of us gathered at Jesus' feet, and pulled at his legs, pulling at the rivets that held the lower portion of the plate to the wall.

Soon Jesus was hanging above us at an odd angle, the crucifix ripped partially down, the plate coming with it, and a section of the wall came off with the plate, exposing an opening that yawned beyond. Latura probed it with his flashlight.

"There's another room back here," Latura said. "Come on!"

Vincent led the way and the Crightons followed, climbing in through the hole we'd torn in the wall, even as straggler rats rushed in with them.

But Latonya was standing on a pew, shaking her head no, while Roger continued cradling his dead wife in his arms. And Mikey stood near his adopted family, waiting for Roger to get it together. I wasn't sure he ever would.

Latura went over to him. Put a hand on the man's shoulder.

"Roger . . . we have to go. You have to leave Eleanor behind."

"I can't . . . can't just *leave* her here!"

"Do you think her last wish was for you to die down here, too?"

Mikey said, "He's right, man. She wanted everybody she loved to live *forever*."

Jackhammers pounded, echoed; the surge of water continued.

"This is a holy place," Latura said. "A spiritual place. Leave her, Roger."

"*She'll* live forever," Roger said, nodding, placing her gently on the pew. The water below was rising, but the pew was dry enough now. "Don't you think she'll live forever?"

"Yes," Latura said, taking his arm, tugging him, "yes. Now let's get the hell out of here!"

Roger and Mikey moved toward the hole behind Jesus, and I took Latonya by the arm. "He's right—we gotta *go*, girl!"

But she was frozen on her perch, petrified. "I can't. I can't do it. No way I'm goin' with all them squiggly-ass rats!"

I yanked her off the fucking pew. "Come on, woman! We'll name the little assholes as we go!"

And I dragged her, and by the time we got to Jesus, she was with the program, and up through the hole into the blackness of the next stratum of hell.

13

STAIRWAY TO HEAVEN

Escaping the chapel through the hole they'd forged in the altar wall, the survivors squeezed through a passageway whose walls consisted of raw, stratified clay, a mud canyon they shared with scampering rats, whose lead they followed, taking a dogleg right into a long forgotten room dating to the tunnel's original excavation.

As the survivors huddled together, Latura sent his flashlight beam exploring.

Carved from the slimy, decomposing Hudson River bed, the massive clay-walled room, with its heavy, hand-hewn support beams and open wood-beam ceiling, workbenches strewn with wrenches and other tools, racks of greased fuse, and wooden crates of blasting caps, had obviously been some kind of staging area for the tunnel's construction. Even an old steam drill, half-covered in sluff, sat tucked against one wall. Most important, a staircase rose twenty feet to a land-

ing, then another twenty to the mouth of a timber-reinforced mine shaft up top.

And it was up those steps, toward that mine shaft, that the mass of instinct-driven rats were swarming.

MADELYNE THOMPSON

Good as it felt to be in an actual *room,* of any kind, this ancient workshop had a musty, ghost-town feel, and despite the massive wooden beams, it was none too stable. Our *world* was none too stable, not with that continual, increasingly deafening jackhammer bludgeoning.

It seemed no sooner had we found ourselves in this seemingly solid chamber than massive chunks of ceiling beam began to fall, under that jackhammer barrage, the walls shaking, too, and as if this man-induced earthquake weren't enough, freezing riverwater began spilling in from the passageway we'd come through. The chapel must have been completely flooded now.

But Latura was shining his flashlight up that endless stairway, where rats darted up, fur glistening, tails flashing.

"That way," Latura said, gesturing to the stairs where the rats scampered upward.

Latonya was still at my side. "No way I'm goin' up there. I hate those little mothers!"

"Normally I'd agree with you," Latura said casually. "But our furry little friends know what they're doing."

"Ain't *my* damn friends!" Latonya insisted.

"Right now," Latura said, "they're the best friends we ever had."

All of us were hesitant to climb those stairs, and it wasn't just the rats that made us pause: that staircase was shaking like funhouse steps, anchor beams slip-sliding in its claylike pistons while the jackhammer pounding kept up its relentless pummeling.

Latura started the climb, testing the stairs, but as water continued rushing in at an alarming rate, there was no time to wait for the outcome of the test.

Steven Crighton stayed at the bottom, helping everyone, steadying them, guiding them onto the stairway.

Then we were scaling the collapsing stairway that rose to God-knew-where. Latura stayed in the lead, with Latonya and Vincent just behind him; Roger was helping Mikey up, and Sarah had her arm around Ashley, who'd gone mildly catatonic, though she still clutched her precious video camera, even if taking footage had long since stopped being a priority for the girl.

"Ready?" Steven asked me.

I gripped the rail. "Why do I think if I don't climb these steps, they're going to climb me?"

Steven smiled and guided me up the first few steps.

The instability, the sponginess of the stairs, didn't exactly inspire confidence. Steven was coming up behind me when a powerful quake, as if the tunnel below were making one last effort to buck us off, rocked the staircase. In front of me, Latonya grabbed onto the handrail for support and it cracked like a wooden matchstick.

"God!" I cried, seeing her lose her balance, reaching out for her, but I wasn't close enough.

Vincent was, God bless him, and he pulled her back, and she regained her footing, but the extra weight sent Vincent cracking down through a collapsing step, sinking, caught there by his armpits, crying for help.

Steven flashed by me and suddenly he and Latonya were helping Vincent up and out through the splintered stair, and all three were soon scrambling up onto the landing between the two flights.

Latura, who'd made it to the top, was coming back down to help people up. The room we were rising through was coming apart, chunks of ceiling, beam, dirt boulders, and rock raining down like a meteor shower, and riverwater was climbing the stairs beneath us now, quickly, inexorably.

Somehow we all made it to the top, at the mouth of a mine-shaft-like hallway, and looked down as the bottom half of the staircase ripped away, sinking into the rising flood-water.

"Do you hear that?" Ashley said, looking down the mine shaft, pointing. "That's traffic! I hear *traffic*!"

And, no kidding, there was light at the end of the mine-shaft tunnel; not much—but light.

"This *is* the way out!" Steven said.

Moving up from behind, where he'd helped us all up, Latura said, "All present and accounted for—let's do it!"

But as if in answer, or rather in contradiction, of what he'd just said, a sound came echoing up from the mangled stair-way.

Barking.

We clustered at the mouth of the staircase and looked down and there he was: Cooper, swimming at the jagged edge of the landing, where the bottom stairs had been torn away, not able to navigate himself up and on. If he could have, he could have scampered up the remaining steps like just another big rat.

But he barked and howled and whined like a child, and maybe he was just a dog, but it was a pathetic, heartbreaking sight nonetheless.

"Hell," Latura said. "I mean, I have *cats*."

"You're not considering . . ." I began.

But before I could finish, Latura, his face a grim mask of resignation, had hustled back down the strained, swaying half-a-staircase. He crouched at the landing, reached out a hand, and Cooper swam to him, closer, closer, and finally Latura had him, scooping him out of the water, where the dog shook the water off himself, spritzing Latura, and streaked up the stairs, right into Mikey and Roger's waiting arms.

"*Now* can we leave?" Latura asked disgustedly, and started back up that shaky half stairway.

We were laughing in relief and joy when a huge chunk of ceiling beam plummeted toward Latura, who saw it coming and ducked to one side, but the damn thing crashed right through the staircase, tearing, splintering, destroying, severing all but the half flight to the top, and Latura tumbled into the flood tide, as more ceiling fragments rained around him, and he swam frantically to the wall near the partial stairway, but his fingers just clawed uselessly at the slick clay.

Treading water, he called up to us. "Keep going! This'll float me up, and in time I'll make it. But you get the hell *going*—now!"

"Not without you!" I called down to him.

"No!"

Without thinking, I moved down the few hanging stairs and got to the last one and reached out to him, even though he was a good ten feet away.

Then Steven was next to me, handing me a rope of sorts he'd fashioned by knotting together his sweater and shirt. I floated it out toward Latura, but he couldn't reach it, not at first anyway, then he stroked closer, fighting the current, closer . . .

. . . and the stairway gave completely away!

Steven had hold of me with one hand, and somehow he'd managed to grab onto the edge of the mine-shaft landing; I guess some of the others were bracing him, because he didn't fall.

But he couldn't hold on to me, and my wet hand went

slickly sliding through his equally wet grasp, and I went tumbling into the rising water, splashing back into that cold filthy bath, and then Latura was beside me, Kit was beside me, holding on to me, saying what a fool I was.

We looked up and could see that a dismayed, bare-chested Steven had been pulled by the others to safety up on the landing.

"She's all right!" Kit called. "I've got her! Steven, you gotta keep 'em going! Go! Go!"

"Not without you two!" Steven yelled.

"We can't leave you!" Latonya was saying, and the others overlappingly said the same.

God, it was cold, so cold it almost didn't feel wet anymore, and I couldn't make myself say anything. I wanted to tell them to go. Kit, holding on to me, treading water with me, did it for me.

"Listen to me! We've come this far. That's home base up there. Slide in, *now*! Go for it!"

Even blinking Hudson River water out of my eyes, I could see that that mine shaft was trembling around them; the well-intentioned but deadly jackhammering was going to collapse that, too. They had to go!

Sarah Crighton, her arm around the stunned-looking Ashley, said, "We can't just leave you—not after everything you've—"

"We'll see you up top," Kit said. "Meet you for breakfast! We'll float up, and be right behind you, but dammit, this is no time for waiting!"

Noting the trembling beams around him, Roger Trilling, with Mikey and Cooper next to him, said, "What if this mine shaft goes? How will you get out then?"

"Hey, I'm making it up as I go along," Kit said, spitting out water. "Steven, get them the hell out of here!"

Steven nodded, and paid Kit respect by obeying his com-

175

mand. Soon the opening of the mine shaft was empty. We were alone.

And then the world around us was racked by a terrible set of quakes; I held on to Kit, hugged him as he treaded water for both of us.

Then it was over.

But the mouth of the mine shaft was gone. The whole shaft had apparently collapsed, and we could only hope our friends had made it somewhere safe in time.

As for us, we were sealed in.

"I'm okay," I gasped, sputtering water, "I can manage."

I could tread water on my own, now. But I still stayed close to him.

"I thought they'd never leave," he said with mock disgust.

My teeth were chattering. "Y-y-you . . . you never g-g-give up, do you?"

"Not in my nature. Hey, at least the rats are gone. Listen, I'm gonna go under and check out those workbenches. See what I can come up with. Don't go anywhere."

"I'll try n-n-not."

He dove under. He seemed to be gone forever, but it was probably less than a minute. When he resurfaced, he had a coil of fuse and a blasting cap.

"You know," he said, "I haven't blown anything up for a while."

"G-g-getting itchy, are you?"

"How long can you hold your breath?"

"L-l-long as it t-takes."

"Right answer."

"I m-m-make 'em up as I go along."

He grinned, then his eyes narrowed. "Get a good breath. We're going back."

"B-back?"

"To the tunnel."

He sucked in a huge breath, and I did the same, and he dove under, and I followed, stroking beside him, as he charted a course with his flashlight, down through the workshop chamber, through the clay-walled passageway, back through the hole into the chapel where the clay Jesus was dissolving to reveal a rusted wire frame. We stroked back down through the hatchway, past the hanging pictures of tunnel workers, up the stairs into the now completely flooded guard booth, and out a busted window into the tunnel, air bubbles trailing, both of us running out, until we burst to the surface, gasping for breath.

And to do that, to get that lungful of thin lousy air, we had to cock our heads sideways, because the water level was now only nine inches from the ceiling of the tunnel.

"N-n-now what?" I asked. Fair question, I thought.

In here, the jackhammering had a weird, tubby echo.

"We're going to blow out of here," he said, his water-streaked face inches from mine.

The panic was setting in; I couldn't help it.

" 'B-blow out'? What the hell does *blow out* m-mean?"

"Come on," he said, and gestured with his head and side-stroked off, and I grunted and followed him.

Swimming on our sides, just under the ceiling, we weren't moving very fast. And our faces were out of the water, facing each other, so we could carry on a conversation of sorts.

"Where are we h-h-heading?" I asked him.

"The mudslide."

So that was our destination: that mud dam we'd created eons or years or hours ago. Whenever.

We cocked our heads so we could breathe what little air there was. And as we side-swam he explained his strategy.

"We're about a hundred feet under," he said. "There's

enough atmosphere buildup in here to shoot us up through the riverbed and out—like a geyser."

"What? Like Old Fuh-Faithful?"

"Just like that."

"Only Old Fuh-fuh-Faithful goes off on schedule."

"Sure. That's why they call it Old Faithful. So?"

"So you d-d-don't even know *when* this'll b-blow."

"That's why we're going to give it a little jump start."

He paddled on. So did I.

Sucking moments of life from our nine-inch airspace.

GRACE LINCOLN

I was sitting in the control room, staring at my dead monitors, when Norm came in, and over to my station. I turned and looked up at him, hoping against hope, but even before I asked, "Anything?" I knew there wasn't, from his tired, defeated demeanor.

"Come on," he said. "Let's let the fresh crew in. I'll buy you breakfast. We'll take my car."

I gave my dead monitors one last look, then I nodded, said, "Okay."

Dawn was filtering in the windows of the garage as we headed for Norm's Buick. We weren't saying anything. Between the jackhammering Scorpions and rumbling wreckers rolling back into the garage, there wasn't much point. Besides, what was there to say?

"Oh, shit!" Norm said.

I heard that.

"What?" I asked.

"Damn rats! I hate those bastards. Where did *they* come from?"

And there they were, a little troop of wet rats, scurrying across the cement.

Wet rats . . .

"Look," I said, pointing.

Their number was increasing—hell, they were *streaming* out of the darkness, leaving a wet slimy trail, but that trail pointed to where they'd come from, a grating in one corner.

I grabbed a broom and moved toward them, swatting them out of my way as I went.

And I heard a voice, from below, echoing up, a child's voice, a male child.

"Hey! Is anybody there?"

Beneath the grating, looking up through its crosshatch grid, were the moist, shining, smiling faces of the little group that has come to be known in the media as the Manhattan Tunnel Survivors.

Norm hadn't made the journey with me; he hadn't grasped the significance of a bunch of wet rats.

So I gave my boss an order, screamed it at him, actually: "Get one of those damn wreckers over here, now!"

14

BLOWOUT

Grace Lincoln made her discovery in the garage of the control-room building shortly after dawn; within seconds a wrecker had backed up to that corner, and within seconds of that a chain attached to the wrecker's winch ripped the grating right out of the concrete.

A trio of paramedics, summoned by Grace Lincoln's cellular phone, had rushed in and were waiting beside the grating hole to lean down and help the survivors up and out of there, to the accompaniment of approaching, wailing sirens. Lincoln and her supervisor, Norman Bassett, moved in to help as one by one the wet, tattered band of intrepid disaster victims was lifted up into daylight, their smudged, occasionally bruised and nicked faces shining brighter than the sunny, unseasonably warm day that awaited them.

First up was the youngest and smallest, Miguel Valdez, then the two teenage girls, Ashley Crighton and Latonya

Washington, followed by another teenager, Vincent Hernandez; then the adults, Sarah Crighton, moving immediately to her daughter, and Roger Trilling, who first lifted his dog up to one of the rescue workers, and finally bare-chested Steven Crighton.

As the paramedics wrapped each of them in space blankets (even the gleefully barking dog got one), they hugged each other indiscriminately, laughter and tears, joy and sorrow, echoing through the cement garage.

GRACE LINCOLN

It may sound selfish—and don't think I wasn't thrilled—that my heart wasn't leaping with joy at the sight of these survivors, but when I realized there was nobody else down there, nobody else coming up, I had to ask.

They were huddled together in their blankets, grinning, weeping, some of them hopping up and down out of trying to get warm and out of sheer excitement.

"There was a tunnel cop down there," I said to them. "His name's George Tyrell. . . ."

From the way their faces fell, I didn't need any further answer.

But the girl whose name I later learned was Latonya Washington said, "He was with us . . . helpin' us . . . but you know, he . . ." She couldn't say it. Instead she said, "Ain't no way we could of make it, without his helpin' us."

I leaned against Norm and he slipped a supportive arm around my shoulder.

"What about Latura?" Norm asked them.

The bare-chested man—Steven Crighton—stepped forward, as if he were the group's official spokesperson. He said, "*He* got us out."

Then he glanced over at the hole in the cement floor where the grating had been torn away.

"Gave his life to do it," he said.

And then he broke down, covering his face, sobbing; his daughter went to him, and then his wife did, too, comforting him.

I didn't cry. I was too numb. And I was still in my professional mode, you know? I'd save my tears for my own damn time. So I just smiled. Happy for them. Happy for us, too, because we had our survivors up and out of there.

What I didn't know—and neither did our hardy little band of tunnel evacuees—was that we still had two more down there.

MADELYNE THOMPSON

The cold was even getting to Kit now; his teeth were chattering as badly as mine, as we sidestroked under the tunnel roof, so close to it our heads and bodies were scraping it now. I wondered if his arms felt as heavy as mine did— every stroke, they seemed to weigh more.

"Has . . . has anyone ever survived a b-blowout b-b-before?"

"Sure," he said, too casually. "When they were d-digging the Baltimore Tunnel last year, two workers blew clean out."

"What huh-happened to them?"

His expression was deadpan. "Not a scratch."

"K-Kit . . . I'm tired . . . can we rest?"

"No."

Finally, after a million more agonizing strokes, swimming with leaden arms, we reached the mud dam, where the tunnel ceiling had broken away enough for Kit to claw his way up and out of the water, and sit himself on the edge of the fractured roof. He reached down and scooped me up and drippingly out and sat me down beside him.

We held each other tight. No romance in it; we were shivering, rubbing each other to keep up circulation, to share whatever little body heat we had remaining.

"Come on," he said, pushing me away a little, "we have to keep moving. . . ."

But I was feeling so drowsy. "Maybe we could just rest a minute—"

"No! It's hypothermia. That's what killed Eleanor. Don't give in to it!"

He shook me, forcibly, like an abusive parent shaking a naughty child, and hauled me to my feet—the roof of this little room was, of course, the cast-iron tube itself—and he rubbed my shoulders and my back, as if he were trying to spark a fire.

But I was *so* sleepy. . . .

"Stay *with* me, Madelyne! Fight it. Fight it!"

I wasn't even so awfully cold anymore. There was a pocket of warmth in front of me, I could almost see it, if I just let go, I could ease down into it and curl up, like in my own warm bed back in Indiana. . . .

That was when he kissed me.

It was a hard kiss, yet it was tender, and maybe it was what I'd been waiting for, because my eyes snapped open, like I'd just got my wake-up call.

"We're almost out of time," he said.

"Pretty b-bold," I said. "T-t-taking liberties like that . . ."

"You want dinner first?"

"No. B-b-breakfast."

Then I kissed him back. Not hard. Just a tiny affectionate gesture, and then I said, "I'm with you. I'm okay."

Beneath us, an earthquakelike tremor shook the tunnel, making it shudder, as the vast pressures within shifted.

"These are my last babies," Kit said, standing away from me, slapping together three bricks of plastic explosive as if they were modeling clay. He inserted a blasting cap and crimped the fuse he brought along from that workshop chamber.

"What if it d-doesn't work?"

He shrugged. "Rain check on breakfast?"

I managed a weak little smile, and so did he.

Then he stuck the hand bearing that explosive wad deep into the muck, armpit-deep. It came back brown and sludgy.

"I better wash this off," he said, and nodded toward the freezing water just below the fractured ceiling.

"You mean . . . ?"

"Yeah. We have to go back down there. Way down."

I swallowed. "I don't k-know if I can do it. . . ."

He put his hand under my chin as my teeth chattered. "I *know* you can do it," he said. "We're a team. Just stay with me."

And he held me, hugged me. For warmth. For strength.

That jackhammering seemed to go suddenly ballistic—had they broken through?

Beneath us the tunnel shuddered with a terrifying seismic intensity that paled every prior quake, and the world went out from under us, the ceiling we'd been standing on collapsing into a pile of rubble, and we were so much more rubble pouring down into the icy waters as ceiling fragments splashed and drifted around us like ice-floe chunks.

Startled by the cold, I realized we had actually gotten warmer up on that ceiling, and as we treaded water there, with more headroom at least now that the ceiling was gone, Kit withdrew a small plastic Ziploc from his vest. In the Ziploc were magnesium/phosphorus matches and strikers.

"Keep trying," Kit said, but he wasn't talking to me. He was talking to the tunnel; his eyes were wild, and this was as close to losing it as he'd come, on this journey. "You think you can kill us? Keep trying! Go ahead! Only we're going to kill you *first*. . . . I'm gonna blow your fuckin' heart right out of your body!"

And he lighted two matches. They burned with an incredible intensity and his face had that same lumpy beautiful dignity in their orange glow.

"Ready?" he asked me.

"With you—anytime, anywhere," I said.

And he touched the matches to the fuse.

"Grab a lungful," he advised, and I did and so did he, and we plunged below the surface.

Down we stroked, down along the mud wall, down to the roadbed where cars protruded from the muck like half-buried artifacts of some ancient time, a strange murky world Kit's flashlight partly illuminated, a weird reminder of something that used to be.

Kit grabbed on to a door handle, and with his flashlight tucked under his armpit, he used his other hand to pull me around, and nodded upward, and I could see, we could both see, the orange streaking of the fuse as it traveled ever upward, getting more faint as it sought its own end.

Then the tunnel shifted again, and a mini-avalanche of mud rained down and covered me like a mudpack from hell, coating me, clutching me, until only my head was sticking out, as if I'd been buried in sand, and I felt the hysteria rising in me even as the air bubbles trailed from my lips. I wanted to scream, but I couldn't, that would only drown me, and kill me even sooner, mud, clammy mud trapping me, holding me, Kit frantically scooping at the ooze, but it had me, and the more leverage he tried for, the more his hands got embedded themselves, as if he were trying to dig me from tar.

Writhing in that awful muck, I felt a terror I'd never known, not even in this long terrible night, and I knew I was going to die and a mudslide of fear within my mind was starting to blot everything out.

Stupidly, I gave in to the urge to scream, but all that accomplished was letting water in, and I swallowed it, and began to choke, until Kit's hand closed over my nose and mouth.

If he hadn't done that, I'd have drowned right then.

He frowned at me, telling me not to panic, and I tried to find the will to follow his lead as I watched him open the door of that nearby car. A *New York Post* floated out, drifted flutteringly by, like some surreal tropical fish, as Kit leveraged all his weight through his legs, thrusting back, and— *yes!*

He yanked me free, in a cloud of silt.

His timing was impeccable, because above us, that plastic explosive erupted with a million pounds of lift, its flash sending shock waves toward us, the water around us beginning to roll, and roil, with brute force.

He hugged me desperately to him, locking me in his embrace, locking my eyes with his, nodding to me as our hair streamed upward with the air bubbles: *the blowout had begun.*

A swirling tide bounced off the roadbed, rocketing back toward the tube in the water equivalent of an updraft, catching us wrapped in our tight embrace, sending us rocketing up toward the tube!

The upthrust carried us through the breach Kit's explosive had blown, sending us past the tunnel's cast-iron shell, caught in a new tunnel, a tunnel of thrusting water that cleaved the very riverbed, making a path for us, seeking, searching for release, carrying us like two frail bubbles up, up, up through the alluvium, splitting it, clearing the way as the great geyser sought release.

Clutched in our embrace, we rode, caught within the liquid

torpedo as it tore through the rifting, splitting river bottom, its force driving on relentlessly against all resistance, shooting us like a bullet through billowing clouds of silt . . .

. . . and we helped, kicking upward as we shot through the water, clasping each other desperately, becoming one person, one flesh-and-blood projectile, as above us—*light*—the surface of the river coming closer and closer, bright and brighter, until that was all we could see.

Or were we already dead? Was this that light at the end of the tunnel that those who've nearly died, and come back, have reported? We were heading into afterlife?

Or life?

Then, through the roiling, swirling river surface, we came, the blowout propelling, shooting us through, the frigid winter wind suddenly, sweetly, on our faces as we sucked air, fresh air, real air, deep into our lungs, polluted New York, Hudson River air, and nothing had ever smelled better.

Then we were bobbing on the surface of the river, our embrace intact, and I looked at his face, his smiling face, smiling in a way he'd never shown me down below, and I showered him with kisses.

"You're pretty easily impressed," he said, between kisses. "I don't usually get this far on first dates."

And we treaded water there, arms around each other's waist, watching as Coast Guard cutters and police cruisers—against a sublimely beautiful backdrop of the lower end of Manhattan, World Trade Towers, Battery Park, and its boats—came racing toward us.

The sun was still rising. We were in the midst of a dawn rising over the cityscape in all its pale, wintery glory.

Daylight.

Before long, we were aboard a harbor rescue skiff, sitting wrapped in astronaut blankets, huddled together, heading back to New Jersey. We each had our own personal EMS paramedic to check our cuts and nicks and bruises.

I took Kit's bandaged hand in my bandaged hand and said, "Thanks."

"Just doing my job."

"Not really. You resigned, remember."

He shrugged. "I resigned the position. Not the job."

"I'm going to try again."

"What?"

"I say 'Thanks,' you say . . ."

And I gestured for him to fill in the blank.

Another smile. "You're welcome."

"There! That wasn't so hard, was it? I mean, you've pulled off tougher assignments."

A little laugh. "Still planning to leave New York?"

"I haven't given that much thought. I've been . . . preoccupied lately."

"Ah."

"I don't really know. Suddenly I have options. Maybe New York's got other things in mind for me, and all of this was just, you know . . . a gentle hint I should stick around. Or maybe not. Either way, I think I may have finally overcome my fear of rats."

"Think so?"

"Except maybe the ones I wind up dating."

He looked away from me. He seemed suddenly ill at ease.

"Hey," I said. "Back in the Midwest, we call that an opening."

"Look . . . you're under no obligation. . . ."

"Obligation?"

He shrugged. He clearly felt awkward about this. "People meet in certain kinds of tense situations, and form a kind of . . . bond. Self-preservation brings people together. . . ."

"And then when it's over, they have nothing in common? It's a kind of a false friendship, a temporary relationship?"

He shrugged again. "Can be."

"I thought we agreed 'no bullshit.' "

Tiny grin. "I guess we did."

"And you promised me something."

"I did, didn't I."

"So are you going to ask, or do I have to?"

"Would you like, uh—"

"Yes. I would. Breakfast would be delightful. I've worked up an appetite, somehow."

"Start with breakfast," he said, "and take it from there?"

"Yes. One step at a time. Make it up as we go along."

And I kissed him again, softly, tenderly.

"Can I make a suggestion?" he asked.

"Sure."

"In the future—can we take the bridge?"

And we held each other and laughed.

EPILOGUE

The skiff bearing Madelyne Thompson and Kit Latura docked at a rotting wharf near the Colgate Clock, near an old boat shack, a destination chosen to keep the two away from the media for the moment.

Awaiting them as they disembarked were Deputy Chief Frank Kraft, Control Room Supervisor Norman Bassett, Grace Lincoln, and Cathy Dix, as well as several EMS paramedics.

CATHY "BOOM" DIX, EMS

All I said to Chief Latura was, "I knew it would take more than this to kill a stubborn son of a bitch like you," and all the chief said was, "Cathy, you're a sentimental slob."

But there was this nice moment between Deputy Chief Kraft and the chief. Has anybody told you about that? No? Well, then . . .

Deputy Chief Kraft just goes up to the chief and flings a green EMS parka over his shoulders, takes his arm, and leads him toward the base camp by the New Jersey River Building.

"Triage is this way," Kraft says.

"No shots," the chief says. "You know how I hate shots."

And this is the nice moment.

The deputy chief says to him, "You're the boss."

Oh, and I guess I forgot to mention—that parka Kraft slung around Latura's shoulders, it had a word stenciled on it in big bold letters: CHIEF.

GRACE LINCOLN

Well, later, Kit Latura and I sat and talked, but that morning, at the dock, when he and Madelyne Thompson got off that skiff, with Norm and Deputy Chief Kraft and Boom and a bunch of others around, we didn't say a word to each other.

He just took my hand and pressed the bracelet in it.

We looked at each other for a second, and then Deputy Chief Kraft ushered him and Ms. Thompson over to base camp.

Norm was at my side. "You okay?" he asked.

"Yeah," I said. "I don't suppose you still got that bottle handy?"

He touched my shoulder. "I'll pour some in your coffee. Let's go get some breakfast."

And we did.

They put us in this tent and give us soup and hot coffee and stuff, and we wrapped in blankets and at first we be real happy, then sort of get depressed, thinkin' about the ones we left behind, you know?

But then some people come in and say Kit Latura and Madelyne, they got blowed out into the river, some way, and they comin' back on a boat, right now, alive and kickin'!

Well, after that, I never seen a happier bunch of people, and just so you know, we stay friends, all of us. Mikey and Vincent and me, we all got time off for good behavior, we was only at the work camp maybe two weeks, and Sarah Crighton is helpin' me get some trainin' and she say I gone get Nordell back, if I get a job and stay off the street, and ain't no way I be back sellin' myself. Rather go back down in that damn tunnel.

Anyway, gettin' ahead of things.

We be sittin' in that tent, all happy and shit, and Steven Crighton come runnin' in, sayin', "Here they come!"

And draggin' our blankets and our sorry behinds, we go runnin' up to Kit and Madelyne, huggin' 'em and shit. All of us in one great big hug, huggin' each other, but mostly huggin' Kit.

'Cause Kit, he the one come down and save our asses, and maybe our souls, too, who knows?

"They oughta give you a medal, man," I say.

And he say, "Seein' your faces is all the medal I need."

Well, of course they offer him his job back, too, even though some stupid people bitch about how he blew up city property and shit? But he turn 'em down.

He got a better job, doin' the same kind of emergency stuff. Only out in California. No tunnels, plenty of daylight, and besides, his wife's writin' a movie about us.

Bet you can guess her name.

MAX ALLAN COLLINS has earned an unprecedented seven Private Eye Writers of America "Shamus" nominations for his "Nathan Heller" historical thrillers, winning twice (*True Detective,* 1983, and *Stolen Away,* 1991).

A Mystery Writers of America "Edgar" nominee in both fiction and nonfiction categories, Collins has been hailed as "the Renaissance man of mystery fiction." His credits include five suspense-novel series, film criticism, short fiction, songwriting, trading-card sets, and occasional movie/TV tie-in novels, including such best-sellers as *In the Line of Fire, Dick Tracy, Maverick, Waterworld,* and *NYPD BLUE: Blue Beginning*.

He scripted the internationally syndicated comic strip *Dick Tracy* from 1977 to 1993, is cocreator (with artist Terry Beatty) of the comic-book feature *Ms. Tree,* and has written both the *Batman* comic book and newspaper strip. His most recent comics project is *Mike Danger* for Tekno-Comix, co-created with best-selling mystery writer Mickey Spillane.

Collins directed, wrote, and executive-produced *Mommy,* a suspense film starring Patty McCormack and Jason Miller, debuting on home video in 1995, and was screenwriter of *The Expert,* a 1995 HBO World Premiere film. Several Collins-scripted films are now in preproduction from the author's midwestern company, M.A.C. Film Productions.

Collins lives in Muscatine, Iowa, with his wife, writer Barbara Collins, and their teenage son, Nathan.